REA

ALLEN COU

P9-ECS-926

3 1833 05142 6036

Long-stemmed candlesticks flanked an arrangement of fresh flowers in the center. Never in Serena's wildest dreams had she imagined a man would pamper her so. Jake must be really serious about her. The ramifications of that thought made her heart skip a little faster.

The most she'd ever got from a boyfriend before was a packet of peanuts thrown across the pub table after he'd been to the bar. In her experience, musicians who knew she had a rich father didn't bother frittering their hard-earned cash on her. Quite the opposite. But it wasn't the quality of Jake's chinaware that impressed her. It had taken time and careful thought to create all this—just for her. It was utterly seductive.

Jake was shaping up to be Mr. Right.

ROMANCE

JAN 0 5 2007

FIONA HARPER

As a child, Fiona Harper was constantly teased for either having her nose in a book or living in a dream world. Things haven't changed much since then, but at least in writing she's found a use for her runaway imagination. After studying dance at university, Fiona worked as a dancer, teacher and choreographer, before trading in that career for video editing and production. When she became a mother she cut back on her working hours to spend time with her children, and when her littlest one started preschool she found a few spare moments to rediscover an old but not forgotten love—writing.

Fiona lives in London, but her other favorite places to be are the Highlands of Scotland and the Kent countryside on a summer's afternoon. She loves cooking, good food and anything cinnamon flavored. Of course, she still can't keep away from a good book, or a good movie—especially romances—but only if she's stocked up with tissues, because she knows she will need them by the end, be it happy or sad. Her favorite things in the world are her wonderful husband, who has learned to decipher her incoherent ramblings, and her two daughters.

Blind-Date Marriage is Fiona's debut novel.

Fiona's second book, *Her Parenthood Assignment*
will be published in Harlequin Romance®
in March next year.

Blind-Date
Marriage

FIONA
HARPER

SILHOUETTE *Romance*®

Published by Silhouette Books

America's Publisher of Contemporary Romance

If you purchased this book without a cover you should be aware that this book is stolen property. It was reported as "unsold and destroyed" to the publisher, and neither the author nor the publisher has received any payment for this "stripped book."

 SILHOUETTE BOOKS

ISBN-13: 978-0-373-19843-6
ISBN-10:   0-373-19843-4

BLIND-DATE MARRIAGE

First North American Publication 2006

Copyright © 2006 by Fiona Harper

All rights reserved. Except for use in any review, the reproduction or utilization of this work in whole or in part in any form by any electronic, mechanical or other means, now known or hereafter invented, including xerography, photocopying and recording, or in any information storage or retrieval system, is forbidden without the written permission of the editorial office, Silhouette Books, 233 Broadway, New York, NY 10279 U.S.A.

All characters in this book have no existence outside the imagination of the author and have no relation whatsoever to anyone bearing the same name or names. They are not even distantly inspired by any individual known or unknown to the author, and all incidents are pure invention.

This edition published by arrangement with Harlequin Books S.A.

® and TM are trademarks of Harlequin Books S.A., used under license. Trademarks indicated with ® are registered in the United States Patent and Trademark Office, the Canadian Trade Marks Office and in other countries.

Visit Silhouette Books at www.eHarlequin.com

Printed in U.S.A.

For the unknown man I soaked
while driving through a puddle

CHAPTER ONE

JAKE knew only two things about the woman he was going to meet: her name was Serena and her father had money.

Serena.

Sounded kind of horsey. She probably wore jodhpurs. Mel had refused to comment on whether she was pretty or not, so she probably looked like a horse as well. He could see it so clearly: the gymkhana trophies, the chintzy bedroom. Serena wore her mousy hair in a bun and had too many teeth.

He stepped off the kerb of the busy London street and zigzagged through the gaps in the traffic. Headlights lit up his knees as he squeezed between the bumpers. A horn blared.

That was why he liked to walk. It gave him a sense of freedom in the midst of the cloying traffic. He wasn't about to take orders from anyone, especially not a pole with coloured lights on top.

Once on the pavement again, he stopped to shake the drizzle off his hair. It was more mist than rain, only visible in the orange haloes of the street lamps, but somehow he was wetter than if he'd been hit by big, splashing drops. He was going to look less than perfect when he arrived at the restaurant.

His long strides slowed as he contemplated the evening

ahead. Should he be marching this briskly towards the unknown? Probably not. But he wasn't going to be late. He speeded up to his former tempo. This evening he would be polite, he would be charming, and then he would be high-tailing it out of there as fast as possible.

As long as Serena didn't have a horsey laugh to match her appearance, he could endure the temptation of the pocket-sized window in the restaurant toilet. At least he hoped there was a window. Just for emergencies.

He should have checked.

In future he would do a reconnaissance of any potential venues when forced on blind dates by his meddling little sister.

Not that there was going to be a next time if he could help it.

He was still a bit hazy about how she'd talked him into going on this one. Mel had rung him at work and slipped it into the conversation while he was studying a balance sheet and saying 'mmm' and 'yup' at suitable intervals. Before he knew it, he was meeting a total stranger for drinks and dinner at Lorenzo's.

One day he would have to put his foot down with Mel. She'd been able to wind him round her little finger ever since she'd bestowed her very first smile on him. He was pretty sure she knew he hadn't been listening when she'd arranged this date. Most likely she'd planned the exact timing of her call to maximise his suggestibility.

He cut through a little park in the centre of the square rather than keeping to the busy street. It was a refreshing change from the unrelenting grey of the city. Not that there was much green within the park's wrought-iron railings at this time of year.

At least it smelled like November—acorns and rotting leaves. He took a deep breath and savoured the warm, earthy aroma. That was when he became aware of the tramp, more noticeable by his body odour than his appearance. He might easily have taken him for a forgotten coat on the bench otherwise.

The old man was oblivious to the rain. Saliva trailed from his open mouth down his chin, and the wind rolled an empty beer can to and fro beneath the bench. Jake removed the copy of the *Financial Times* from under his arm and spread a few pages over the man's shoulders and torso, making sure he didn't accidentally touch his coat. Hopefully, by the time the pages were wet through, the old guy would be sober enough to move himself somewhere drier.

He hurried through the park gate and re-entered the rush hour. The restaurant was only a few minutes away now. He didn't go in for that kind of place much. Lorenzo's was an odd choice for horsey old Serena.

According to the brief review he'd read on the internet, the restaurant was a small, family-run affair—nothing special in his book. He preferred places that were obviously exclusive now he could afford them. Give him women with diamonds, men with fat wallets and waiters that bowed any day.

However, the food was supposed to be tasty, and the critic had raved about a cannelloni dish. Not that it would make any difference to Serena. She was probably going to push a couple of lettuce leaves drenched in balsamic vinegar round her plate and complain about how everything went to her rather expansive hips.

The escape window was sounding more tempting with every step. Perhaps he should pop round the back and check the exact dimensions before he went inside?

He was so lost in thought that he didn't see the blocked drain. He didn't see the deep puddle that had collected over the top of it. He also didn't see the sports car driving up behind him.

He did, however, see the great tidal wave as car met puddle. He watched, helpless, as in slow motion tendrils of spray reared up and soaked him from head to foot.

She saw the wall of water in her rear-view mirror and gasped.

She'd been so busy daydreaming about the evening ahead she'd forgotten to manoeuvre round the small pond that always appeared on this corner in bad weather. Without thinking whether it was a good idea or not, she pulled the car to a halt, got out, and ran straight up to the sodden figure on the pavement. He didn't look as if he'd moved at all. He was just staring down at his dripping suit with his arms aloft.

'Oh, my goodness! I'm so sorry—'

He lifted his head and glared at her.

'Are you okay?'

One eyebrow shot up. At least she thought it did. It was hard to tell under the dark hair plastered onto his forehead.

'You're soaked! Let me give you a lift to wherever you were going. It's the least I can do.'

She'd been talking to him for a good fifteen seconds, but suddenly she had the feeling he was only just taking a good look at her. He was staring. Hard. She looked down at her suede boots and ankle-length skirt. Sure, she was getting a little soggy as she stood here in the rain, but it wasn't as she'd come out with her skirt tucked into the back of h[e]r knickers. At least she didn't think she had.

When she looked back up he was smiling. And not ju[st] the polite tilt of the mouth you gave waitresses when the[y] brought you a drink. This was a real one.

A shiver skittered up her spine. That was a great smile. Sh[e] looked a little closer at the face it was attached to.

Nice.

This was one cute guy she'd drenched.

3 1833 05142 6036

'You were saying…?'

She shook herself.

'Yes. It's just—I…I mean it's the least I can do. Drop you off somewhere, that is.'

'That's probably a good idea. I'm not sure I'm in any fit state to go out to dinner like this.'

Her hands flew to her mouth. 'I feel just awful… Well, that settles it, then. I've ruined your evening. I'm dropping you off somewhere dry and warm. No arguments.'

He looked her up and down, a crinkle at the corners of his eyes. 'No arguments from me. Shall we?' He motioned towards the car. 'Nice wheels.'

The drizzle was making a more concerted effort at proper rain, and a drop splashed on her forehead. Without talking further, they both ran to the low-slung metallic blue sports car and climbed inside.

She watched him shake his head and run his fingers through thick dark hair as he sat in the passenger seat. He looked even better with it slicked back. She could see his face properly. How did eyes that cool blue manage to smoulder? And look at that firm jaw. He looked like a man in control of his destiny. She liked that.

'The car's not mine, actually.'

The smile was back. 'What did you do? Steal it?'

'No, of course not. Mine's being repaired. I borrowed this from my…a friend.'

She wasn't about to tell him she was riding round in her father's car. It had mid-life crisis stamped all over it. Not that her father's crazy behaviour had started in his fifties. He'd got a head start in his teenage years, and had never stopped long enough to mature.

She didn't like admitting to her parentage when she met a man who caught her eye. She'd learnt the hard way to keep dear old dad out of the picture until it was safe to drop the bombshell—and even then she was never one hundred per cent sure if *she* was the main attraction.

The smouldering eyes were looking at her intently. 'A friend?'

Drat! He'd spotted the little detour in her explanation.

He sat back in the seat and smiled, a wistful expression on his face. 'That's too bad. Tell him I think he's got great taste in cars…and women.'

She fumbled with the keys in the ignition.

Come on, girl! Think of something sparkling and witty to say! Tell him he's got the wrong end of the stick.

'So, where can I drop you off?'

Great. Really smooth. Well done.

'Great Portman Street. Do you know it?'

'I know someone who lives down that way.' She indicated and pulled away. 'It's not that far from here, is it?'

'No, but in this traffic it could take a good twenty minutes.'

'I know. Sometimes I think it would be quicker if I walked.'

'My opinion exactly.' He pinched at his trouser leg and inspected it. 'Although I can't vouch for it being the drier option.'

She sighed and started to speak, but he warded the words off with a raised hand.

'Please, don't apologise again. You did me a big favour, in fact. I wasn't looking forward to my evening, and you've given me the perfect excuse to bow out.'

'Really?'

'Yes, really. I was destined for a date from hell with a girl that looks like a horse—and I'm not sure whether it's the front end or the back end she most resembles!'

Her laugh was loud and unexpected.

'Well, consider me your knight in shining armour, then,' she added, giggles bubbling under the surface.

He laughed along with her. 'My eternal gratefulness, kind

lady. In fact, I should thank you in some way. How about dinner?'

Since they were sitting at yet another red light, she shot a look across at him. 'Have you forgotten why you're in my car in the first place? You're dripping wet!'

'It wouldn't take me long to get dry and changed. We could nip out somewhere local. We'd be in a public place. You'd be perfectly safe.'

'How do I know that? We've only just met. I don't even know your name.'

'It's Jake.'

'Well, Jake, I still don't know you from Adam—except that your name's not Adam, that is.' Oh, God, she was rambling!

'Then why did you let me in your—I mean your *friend's* car, then? I could be anyone. I could be an axe-wielding maniac, for all you know.'

She went cold. He was right. She'd been so busy feeling bad for him she hadn't even considered basic personal safety. Her voice was braver than she felt when she answered.

'Don't be daft! I rescued *you*, remember? You're a Jake-in-distress. You can't possibly be an axe-wielding maniac!' *Could he?*

Now it was his turn to laugh. Her shoulders untensed, but she stayed quiet and concentrated on the traffic. Quicker than expected, they drew up in Great Portman Street.

'Which one?' She leaned forward and peered down the road. One side was almost entirely occupied by a red brick block of Victorian apartments.

'Right here. Top floor.'

'Very posh.'

She kept her eyes on the road as the car came to a halt. Even without the tell-tale reflection in the windscreen, she'd have sensed he'd turned to face her. Strange, she'd always thought that being able to feel someone's eyes boring into you was a load of poppycock.

'Come inside and have the grand tour.'

'You're very forward, aren't you?'

'I know what I want, and I don't stop until I get it.'

The implication of that sentence made her cheeks burn. She was very proud of the wobble-free voice that came out of her mouth.

'Sorry, Jake-in-distress, I have a prior commitment. Maybe another time.'

'Couldn't you stand him up?'

A reply like that would normally have had her spitting, but he said it with such lazy charm she found herself laughing.

'No.'

But she wanted to. Miraculously, the prospect of an evening with Charles Jacobs seemed even greyer.

'Too bad.' The tone of his voice said he respected her decision more than he cared to admit. 'At least give me your number.'

'Give my number? To an axe-wielding maniac? You must be mad!'

She smiled at him.

He smiled back.

Boy, those smiles got more brilliant with every outing. If she didn't get out of here quick, she was going to change her mind about dinner. Then Cassie would kill her for standing up the 'suitable' man she'd found for her, and that would never do. She was looking forward to the prospect of *another time* with Jake too much.

He reached into his pocket, fished out a business card and scribbled something on the back with a fountain pen.

'Have it your way. Here's *my* number, then.'

She took it from him. Even the little rectangle of card was soggy. She'd done a really good job with that puddle.

He looked her straight in the eye. 'Use it.'

Her gaze collided with his. He was so sure she was going to call. There wasn't a flicker of doubt in his expression. Women probably fell over themselves to follow his every whim on a daily basis. Part of her felt like throwing the card out of the window and into the gutter; the other part wanted to tuck it inside her bra to make sure she didn't lose it.

Her lips pursed. She meant to look peeved, but somehow a small smile escaped.

'Maybe. Goodbye, Jake.'

She put the car into reverse and started to move out of the parking space. Before she had a chance to pull away, he pounded on the window. 'Wait!'

She pressed the button and enjoyed his mounting irritation as the window edged down bit by bit.

'You haven't even told me your name.'

'So I didn't.'

'Well?'

'I get the feeling you're the kind of man who won't let a tiny detail like that stop you. You'll find out—if you want to badly enough.'

With that, she rolled up the window and drove away. She risked a glance in the rear-view mirror and a huge grin spread over her face. He was standing in the street with his mouth hanging open.

She didn't look back. Instead, she tooted the horn and did a little finger wave.

Now, *that* had been smooth!

Stupid, but smooth.

Stupid, because the only reason she hadn't told him her name was the funny reaction it provoked in almost everyone she met. She hadn't wanted to spoil the moment, hadn't wanted the delectable Jake to have the usual set of preconceptions about her.

What had her parents been thinking when they called her Serendipity? It was tantamount to child abuse! She'd been the target of bullies from her first day of school because of her name.

Why couldn't she have been called Sally or Susan? Nice, sensible, traditional names. No one would think Susan was a hippy wild child. And Sally was the kind of girl whose dad worked a nine-to-five job in an office, while her mum baked jam tarts and fussed over the amount of make-up her teenage daughter was wearing.

She sighed.

Daft to run away without telling Jake her name. Now she would have to look all eager and phone him if she was interested. Which she was. She should have given him her number and let him do the running—she'd always liked the old-fashioned idea of being courted.

She turned the corner and headed back towards the restaurant. Perhaps it had been worth not telling Jake her name just to see the look on his face as she drove away. At least she'd have something to smile to herself about if Charles Jacobs turned out to be as yawn-worthy as he sounded.

She looked at her watch as she pulled up outside the restaurant. Only half an hour late. If she smiled, and flipped her long dark hair around a bit, perhaps Charles wouldn't mind.

She hopped out of the sports car, ran inside, and straight up to the small bar that doubled as a reception desk. There were far too many bunches of plastic grapes and straw-covered bottles for the décor to be in good taste, but she didn't care. It was homey.

Someone was loading small bottles of orange juice onto the bottom shelf. She'd recognise that acre-wide Italian rump anywhere!

'Hey, Maria!'

Maria stood up so fast she sent a couple of bottles rolling

across the floor. Her hands flew into the air and she yelled in the general direction of the kitchen, 'Gino! Our girl is here!'

A round, middle-aged man appeared from the door connecting the kitchen to the bar. 'We thought you'd been run over by a bus—didn't we, darling?'

She ducked behind the bar and gave each of them a kiss on the cheek. 'You fuss like an old woman, Gino. Now, tell me—and don't spare my feelings—what's he like?'

Gino made a dismissive wave towards her favourite table by the window. A monstrous potted palm blocked her view. She stood on tiptoe to get a better look.

The table was empty.

She turned round to Gino, eyebrows raised. 'He hasn't shown up yet?'

Gino shook his head, almost overwhelmed by the tragedy, and she swallowed the urge to chuckle.

'Oh, well. Bring me the usual. I'll hang around until nine. I got here late myself, so I can hardly moan.'

He'd better be worth the wait, though! She'd murder Cassie if she'd set her up with a first-class loser again. Her friend knew she was looking to settle down, but couldn't quite get the distinction between *stable and reliable* and *utterly dull*. She'd only agreed to go on this date because it was less hassle than arguing with Cassie about it. If she said no, Cassie would only badger her for a fortnight until she gave in, so she might as well agree and save herself the earache.

Gino brought her a glass of her favourite red wine, and she sat at the table and scanned the rain-swept horizon.

She sat up and smiled as a man in a smart suit with a bunch of flowers passed the window, but he walked straight past the door and into the arms of a waiting blonde outside the tube station. Minutes ticked past. The only other person to enter the restaurant was a small bald man with bad teeth. She whipped up her menu as an impromptu shield and held her breath. Thankfully, he was greeted by a tall woman with equally bad teeth on the other side of the restaurant. She dropped the menu enough to peek over the top, then jumped as Gino appeared, apparently out of thin air.

'There's a message for you. *He* telephoned.'

By the look on Gino's face, it was not good news. She lowered the menu slightly and held her head high. 'Let me have it, Gino.'

'He said he's very sorry, but something came up.'

Something came up! What kind of lame excuse was that? The puff of air she let out lifted her fringe.

'What did he say, exactly?'

'He said he was not able to come, that he's very sorry, and asked you to meet him tomorrow for lunch at Maison Blanc, one o'clock.' Gino wrinkled his nose at the suggestion of anyone eating somewhere other than his establishment, then he grinned. 'But he also said dinner tonight is on him.'

She slapped the menu closed and smiled like a cat.

'In that case, my good friend, it's the caviar to start for me, followed by the priciest entrée Marco can conjure up, and a glass of champagne for everybody in the room.'

Gino winked. 'That's my girl! You show him.'

The nerve of the man. Standing her up, then practically summoning her to lunch the following day, with no thought at all as to whether it was convenient for her. The fact she was free, and could go if she wanted to, had no bearing on the matter. He was an arrogant jerk to assume she was so desperate for a date that she'd trot along at his beck and call.

Not in this lifetime, buster! No way was she turning up tomorrow. He could be the one to sit and fiddle with his cutlery.

Dinner was good, but revenge on Mr Jacobs was even tastier. She enjoyed every bite, because with each mouthful she could hear the ding of a cash register. By the time she had finished her espresso, she was imagining the look on his face when he saw the total. She had a mind to turn up at Maison Blanc tomorrow, just to see him wince as she delivered the news in person.

Perhaps that wasn't such a bad idea after all. She could bat her lashes and give him the *Oops! Silly me! I never was much good at maths* routine. The added bonus would be that Cassie couldn't moan at her for not giving the latest offering in the husband hunt a fair go.

Thinking of Cassie, it was time to give her an earful. She took her mobile phone out of her bag and punched in the number.

Cassie was never one for pleasantries, and this time was no exception.

'How's it going? Isn't he hot?'

'Not noticeably.'

'Really? I was sure you two would hit it off. My new project worker has talked about her brother so much I feel like he's a long-lost friend.'

'Yeah? Well, he's also my long lost date.'

'What do you mean?'

'He didn't show, Cassie! Some sorry story and an instruction to have dinner on him. You can tell your friend that she'd better get as much visiting time in with her brother as she can, because he's going to have a heart attack when he sees his credit card statement.'

'Oh…'

'Yes, oh! You'd better be making that famous carrot cake of yours when I come for coffee on Wednesday, or I'll never forgive you.'

'Yes, ma'am.' She knew without a doubt that Cassie had just stood to attention in her living room.

'And no more setting me up on blind dates! Got it?'

'Got it.'

Yeah, right. She could practically hear the cogs whirring in Cassie's brain as she did a mental search for the next poor sucker.

'Try and resist the urge to find me a husband as lovely as yours is. We have very different taste in men, remember? I never could understand why you used to moon over the geeks with plasters holding their glasses together in school.'

'Darren Perkins was a god!'

'Of course he was. See you Wednesday—and don't forget the carrot cake. Bye.'

She sighed. If the truth be told, she was pleased her blind date hadn't turned up. But that didn't stop her fuming over her wasted evening. She could have taken Jake up on his offer of dinner. She looked at the phone sitting in her hand. She could still call him.

Was she really that brave? Wouldn't it sound a little desperate if she called him now?

He'd have had time to get in, have a shower and change into something dry. She could picture him padding around a smart flat with polished wood floors, low-slung jeans resting on his hips, his hair damp and smelling of shampoo.

She felt in her pocket for the business card and looked at the number. Her heart sank. The ink had bled into the damp card, making Jake's scrawl illegible. She could make out the first two digits—a three and a two. One of the numbers further along looked suspiciously like a seven. Or was it a one?

If she'd believed in fate, she'd have thought it was an omen. But she had outgrown the New Age hocus-pocus her parents had spoon-fed her since birth. She stuffed the card back in her pocket, doubly cheesed off at the invisible Charles.

When she'd finished her coffee she made her way to where Gino was serving at the bar.

'See you soon, Gino. Tell Marco his cooking was superb, as usual, and give my love to the rest of the family—especially Sophia and your adorable little granddaughter.'

Gino's eyes sparkled with pride. 'Sophia says Francesca is sleeping through the night now.'

'Well, you tell Sophia I will be offended if I'm not first on her list of babysitters when she wants to go out for the evening.'

One more hug for Gino and Maria and she was outside, breathing in the cold night air. The rain had stopped and the stars twinkled up above.

Time to go home and plan her next move.

She stood on the pavement and stared at her car, feeling oddly deflated. She'd been excited at the thought of another sparring match with Jake. Now she had no way of contacting him, even if she wanted to give in to temptation and phone him first.

She flumped into the driver's seat of her dad's car and flung her handbag over the passenger seat into the back, not caring where it landed. She pulled the card out of her pocket again and stared at it hard, willing the numbers to come into focus. If anything, they were even more blurry now. There was only one thing for it.

She jammed the keys into the ignition and stepped on the accelerator. She might not know his phone number, but she knew where he lived.

She took the quickest route she knew back to Great Portman Street—unlike earlier, when she'd taken a couple of scenic detours—and arrived there in less than ten minutes. Her parking left much to be desired. There had to be a good foot between the car and the kerb.

She turned the engine off and sat in the dark.

Funny—now she was here, her feet were decidedly icy. Not because of Jake—he was lovely—but because of what he might read into finding her on his doorstep. She was looking for love and commitment, not a fling, and turning up after ten o'clock, uninvited, would be giving a completely different set of signals.

It was exactly because of this kind of impulsive behaviour that she had ended up with some of the most worthless boy-friends in history. She reminded herself she'd turned over a new leaf. No more leaping before she looked, even if the man she wanted to leap onto looked as good as Jake.

She wound down the window and stuck her head out. Soft light glowed in a few of the penthouse windows.

Why did everything have to come down to such an all-or-nothing choice? If only there was another way to reach him. She picked the card up from where she had flung it on the passenger seat.

Of course! Talk about missing the obvious!

She had been so focused on the telephone number on the back of the card she hadn't even thought about turning it over to find his business address. She could wait a couple of days and phone him at work. That wouldn't be too forward.

She flipped the card over and ran her eyes over the classic black font. An accountant. She liked accountants. They were stable, sensible, and nothing like the kind of men she'd learned to shy away from—musicians, actors, tortured artists.

Jake was looking better and better. He was smart and good-looking, and he must be clever. And he might, just might, be the kind of guy a girl could hope to settle down with.

Then she noticed the name along the bottom and almost dropped the card in shock. Charles Jacobs!

Charles?

He'd told her his name was Jake!

She was about to stub the offending card into the ashtray when she stopped. Jake could be a nickname. After all, she wasn't exactly using *her* given name at the moment. She'd started abbreviating it to Serena. It sounded a lot less flower-child and a lot more…well, normal, than Serendipity. She couldn't blame Jake if he wanted to liven up a stuffy name like Charles.

She looked at the card again and smiled.

Well, well. Charles Jacobs.

Lunch tomorrow was going to be fun.

CHAPTER TWO

JAKE walked into Maison Blanc ten minutes early. Being there first gave him the edge. When Serena arrived he'd be calmly seated at one of the little square tables with its crisp linen tablecloth. He'd make sure he had a good view of the entrance, and scrutinise every female who glided through glass door.

Maison Blanc was his kind of place. The décor was white and clean, full of straight lines. No fuss. No frills. The best feature by far was that he knew how big the bathroom window was. He'd fit through it, no problem.

He walked past the bar into the main part of the restaurant and scanned the entire room from left to right—then did a double take.

It was her!

The mystery woman. Here. Now.

He very nearly swore.

The woman he'd spent most of last night trying to forget, while he punched his pillow and ordered himself to sleep, was sitting at a table in the centre of the room, sipping a drink.

Suddenly he didn't know what to do with his hands.

She looked stunning. Her silky brown hair was swept up into a braided ponytail. Her large, almond-shaped eyes were accentuated with smoky make-up and she wore a soft moss-green cardigan open at the throat. He swallowed. Never had a cardigan looked so sexy.

She was warm and vibrant. A perfect contrast to the sterile surroundings. And something about her seemed indefinably exotic. He wondered if she had gypsy blood coursing through her veins.

She'd started to turn her head in his direction, so he dived behind a pillar and stayed there for a few breathless seconds. Then, when he was sure she wasn't looking, he slunk over to the bar and ordered something. He sat there, hunched over his glass, hoping to heaven she hadn't noticed him. But that didn't seem possible. He was sure every molecule in his body was screaming *Look at me* and waving its arms in her direction.

He risked another glance.

She was looking at the menu. He was safe, for now.

An enigmatic smile curled her lips, as if she were remembering a secret joke. In fact, it looked very much as if she were trying not to laugh.

His fingers traced the rim of his tumbler, but it stayed on the bar as he let his mind wander.

Last night, as they'd driven through the crowded London streets, he'd prayed that every traffic light would stay red, just to keep them locked in the private world of her car a few seconds longer. He'd been fascinated by her movements as she drove, hadn't been able to stop watching the little silver bracelet that danced on her wrist as she moved her hand from steering wheel to gearstick and back. Everything she did was fluid and graceful.

He'd even admired the cool way she'd pulled away and left him gaping in the street. It served him right for his lack of finesse. He'd been too sure she was going to call him. Minutes after her departure he'd been pacing round his flat, scorning himself for being so smug. He'd tried desperately to remember if he had any business contacts who could trace the owner of the blue Porsche.

But it looked as if he didn't need to worry about that. She was here. In fact, he didn't need to worry about anything— except, of course, that she would have a ring-side seat to his blind date with Serena.

Serena! He'd almost forgotten about her.

He looked at his watch. Four minutes to go. Time to pull himself together. He couldn't let her find him sitting at the bar all a-jitter. Perhaps the situation could be salvaged by a bit of quick thinking.

He summoned a waiter and asked to be shown to his table. With any luck he'd be seated in the corner, facing the other direction. Maison Blanc was large, and there were plenty of square white pillars to hide behind.

His step faltered as the waiter led him not to the far corner, but straight towards his mystery woman. Rats! He was going to have to walk right past her table. There was nothing for it but to ooze charm and hope the matter of a lunch-date with another woman could be swept aside once he'd claimed her promise of dinner *another time*.

However, his best, knock-her-socks-off smile never made it past the planning stage—mainly because the waiter had stopped at the table and pulled out the chair opposite her.

He just stood and stared.

The waiter fidgeted and she waved him away. Then she smiled at Jake. He wanted to crawl under the table and hide.

'Good afternoon, Mr Jacobs. I'm pleased you could make it—this time.'

'But you're… You can't be…'

'I'm Serena. Pleased to meet you, Charles—or is it Jake?'

He swallowed.

She couldn't be Serena—her teeth were far too lovely.

She cocked her head on one side, waiting. Reading his mind, as it turned out.

'I wore my hair this way just for you,' she said, and turned her head so the ponytail swished towards him. Then she leant forward and lowered her voice to a conspiratorial whisper. 'Just so you could tell which end of the horse was which.'

Something inside him snapped to attention. She knew! She'd been ready and waiting for him, and he'd walked straight in to her little trap.

'Touché,' he said, his voice unusually croaky.

She was really enjoying this. Her eyes were bright and smiling, but without a hint of malice. She wasn't angry, just teasing him, asking him to share the joke.

He held his hands up in surrender. 'Okay, you got me. When did you know?'

She took a sip of her drink.

'Oh, not until *after* you stood me up. I found your business card in my pocket. An amazing coincidence, don't you think? I suppose I could have phoned you this morning and warned you, but the opportunity to have a little fun was too good to pass up.' She stopped and gave him a very genuine smile. 'I can't really be cross, can I? It was my fault entirely. You only cancelled because I drowned you. I suggest we start again. Deal?'

'Deal.' He dropped into the high-backed leather chair and offered her his hand. 'Charles Jacobs. But nobody calls me that any more—except my sister when she's angry with me. My friends call me Jake.'

She clasped his hand and shook it. Hers was small and delicate and unbelievably soft. The smile he'd abandoned earlier returned without his bidding.

'I don't think I need to tell you my name again, do I? I think, after today, you're never going to forget it.'

'You don't look like a Serena.'

'You don't look like a Charles, either. Why Jake?'

'Boys called Charles got punched where I grew up. Some of my friends shortened my last name and it stuck. It was easier, anyway. I'm named after my father, and it was a relief to have a way to tell us apart.'

'You didn't fancy Junior, then?'

Her smile was warm and easy. He didn't mind her teasing him one bit. Somehow it made him feel welcomed—part of an elite club where they were the only two members—rather than putting him on the defensive. People didn't normally get away with ribbing him like this.

'Don't say you think it suits me!'

She wrinkled her nose and shook her head. Her chocolate-brown eyes held him hypnotised. It took the waiter appearing for their drinks order to break the spell.

They both ordered something non-alcoholic. Thank goodness he'd remembered he was driving before he'd downed that Scotch in one! The waiter moved away unnoticed.

'Your turn to spill the beans,' he said.

'Which beans would those be?'

'You could tell me your name.'

She frowned. 'It's Serena. Don't you believe me? Do you think I'm really called Mildred or Ethel?'

'Of course I believe you. I just want to know the *rest* of your name. You can't be just Serena.'

'Why not? Madonna only uses her first name.'

'But she has a last name too—she just doesn't need to use it. The same thing wouldn't work for you. If I tried to look up Serena in the phone book, I'd never find you. You've got to give me a bit more. For all I know you could disappear again, like you did last night, and I'd be none the wiser.'

She looked thoughtfully at the tablecloth. 'Oh. I see.'

'So? Serena…what?'

She leaned back in her chair and crossed her arms. 'Sorry, Charlie, that's on a need-to-know basis only.'

He leant forward and stared straight into her eyes. 'What if I *really* need to know?'

'I'd have to be *really* convinced.' She laughed and waved her hand in the air. 'Telling you my last name is too much of a commitment; I don't like to be tied down. But don't worry. If I think you can handle it, I'll tell you.'

Jake smiled. A girl on his wavelength. No ties. No strings. Just seeing what the future brought, minute by minute. She was right: he would find out her name. He liked her style—she was keeping him on his toes. It was very refreshing.

Talking to her was easy. He hardly noticed the first course slip by. She was funny and articulate, and he found himself talking back in a way that would have surprised his business associates. Sure, he could turn on the charm when it suited him. It was hard-wired into his genetic make-up. He used it as a mirror, reflecting anything that tried to pierce his armour, so no one got below the surface. Yet as he talked to Serena he found himself giving away little snippets of information he didn't normally make public. Nothing big, just stuff he didn't normally share: what book he'd read most recently, what kind of music he liked. Silly things.

Halfway through their main course he stopped eating and watched her butcher her steak. When her mouth closed round the fork, her eyelids fluttered shut and she let out a little sigh of satisfaction. There was an air of primal sensuality about her. And for some reason he wasn't feeling totally civilised himself at the moment, either. It was as if all the layers of varnish he'd carefully applied over the years were peeling away, leaving him feeling like the gawky teenager he'd once been. He should be scared of that feeling.

She looked up at him as she finished chewing her mouthful, her eyes questioning.

'I didn't realise six ounces of sirloin could be so riveting.'

Caught red-handed—or red-faced, to be exact.

He said the first thing that popped into his head. 'I'm just surprised to see you demolishing it with such gusto. You look more of a beansprouts-and-tofu kind of girl to me.' He didn't know why. Perhaps it was the long hair, the intricate earrings that dangled from her ears, or the skirt that swooshed when she crossed her legs.

She dropped her knife and fork and scowled at him.

'I've had enough beansprouts to last me a lifetime, believe me! My parents were dedicated vegans until—' Her breath caught for a second. 'Never mind. Let's just say my love of animal flesh is probably teenage rebellion that's way past its sell-by date.' She grinned. 'Since I was fourteen I've been a true carnivore. In fact, I'd go as far as to say I've never met a bit of cow I didn't like.'

She speared the next piece of steak and blood oozed out of it.

Jake shuddered, unable to tear his gaze away.

'Aren't you going to finish your swordfish?'

He picked up his cutlery and shoved something from his plate into his mouth. He didn't taste what it was. He just had to remind himself to keep cutting and chewing until his plate was empty.

Serena eyed the dessert menu when her plate had been taken away. 'Aren't you having any?'

'Not for me. I don't really eat dessert. I think I'll just have a coffee.'

'Mmm. Perhaps I should too, but that chocolate concoction looks—'

Her mobile phone trilled.

'Excuse me. I forgot to turn it off. I won't be a second.'

'No problem.'

He leaned back in his seat and took the opportunity to study her while her attention was elsewhere.

'Hello? Oh, it's you. I'm sorry, but I'm in the middle of...
No, don't do that! Just stay put, will you? Yes, but... Look!
Just give the phone to Benny... Let me talk to Benny. I'm
not getting any sense out of you...'

She mouthed 'sorry' at him and her cheeks flushed an ap-
pealing shade of pink. He shrugged. It was nice to see he
wasn't the only one who could lose his cool.

'Just keep him there, will you, Benny? I'll be there as soon
as I can... Yes...don't worry... Just don't let him punch
anybody else...'

Jake's ears pricked up.

She snapped her phone closed and exhaled long and hard.

'I'm sorry, I need to go. It's an emergency.'

'Anything I can do to help?'

'No, I'll be fine. I just need to get to Peckham as soon
as possible.'

Peckham? Why on earth was a rich girl like her going
there?

'What for?'

'I've got to find a pub called The Swan.'

She stood up, skirted the table, and gave him an absent-
minded kiss on the cheek. 'Thanks for lunch. I really
enjoyed it.'

And before Jake could argue she'd rushed out through the
door and onto the pavement.

He dug in his pockets for his credit card and paid as
quickly as he could. By the smile on the waiter's face, he
guessed he'd left a ridiculously large tip. But he couldn't be
bothered to do the maths, so he'd just rounded it up to the
nearest hundred.

He shoved the door open and almost bumped into Serena,
who was standing on the kerb, waving her hands around.

'What are you doing?'

'I'm trying to find a taxi! One minute the whole street is

teeming with them; the next minute there's not one to be had for love nor money.'

He pulled her arm down and turned her to face him. Only then did he see the tremble in her lip, her pale face.

'Hey.' He slid his hand down her arm until he found her hand and gave it a squeeze. 'It'll be okay.'

She sniffed. 'I need to get to that pub as soon as I can, or there's going to be a huge amount of trouble!' She pulled away from him and ran to the kerb again as a black cab hurtled past. She looked as if she were about to sprint up the road after it when Jake reached for her again.

'I'll take you. My car's round the corner. I know a way round the back-doubles that'll cut out a lot of the traffic.'

Her eyes gleamed and threatened to overflow. 'Would you really? You don't know how grateful I am. But you've got to promise me something.'

'What's that?'

She grabbed both his shoulders in what, at that time, seemed like an overly dramatic gesture. 'You can't tell a soul about what happens when we get there. It's vitally important.'

Her words haunted him as he turned his car towards the river and headed over Vauxhall Bridge. He left the main roads after passing The Oval, and wove through the back streets. The climbing numbers on the milometer matched his growing unease. He hadn't been back this way for years, had promised himself he never would. He'd done everything humanly possible to claw his way off the high-rise council estate he'd grown up on.

What had she got herself mixed up in? Trouble in this neck of the woods normally meant something criminal. Although she looked unconventional, he hadn't taken her for the kind of woman who courted real trouble. She lacked a certain brand of hardness he was all too familiar with.

But appearances could be deceptive. He'd learned that from his father—living proof that even the tastiest-looking apple could be maggoty at the core.

His eyes flicked over to Serena in the passenger seat. He'd only just met this woman. She could be anyone, involved in anything. For Pete's sake, he didn't even know her last name.

However, his gut said he could trust her, and when he thought of her face when the black cab had sailed past, he knew it was right. Whatever she was involved in, it wasn't drugs or dirty money. She really cared about the man—he presumed it was a man—they were racing to rescue.

A few minutes later he pulled up outside The Swan, or as close as he could get to it. A clampers' lorry was just about to winch a car off the double yellow lines outside.

A metallic blue Porsche.

Blast! He'd forgotten all about the guy with the Porsche. What a prize doughnut he was! He'd raced halfway across London to bail her boyfriend out of trouble. The hairs on the back of his neck bristled as he imagined some T-shirted lout, who obviously didn't look after Serena the way she deserved to be looked after.

Serena jumped out of the car and raced into the pub before he could undo his seat belt. Was she always this impetuous? Or was it just that the Porsche guy was so great she couldn't wait another second to be with him?

His frown deepened and he pulled himself out of his car, straightened his tie, and followed her inside. The smell of stale smoke and beer hit his nostrils as he pushed the door open. This place was even more of a dive than it had been last time he'd been here—and that had to be a good ten years ago. The same torn, faded upholstery covered the stools and benches, only it was even more torn and faded than he remembered.

A couple of blokes with tattoos on their knuckles propped

up the bar. He knew their sort. He couldn't judge them, though. If he'd had a little less luck, made a few different choices, it could have been him standing there, whiling away his dole money on watered-down beer.

He turned his attention to the overturned table and broken glass in the far corner. Serena was leaning over a man sprawled on one of the upholstered benches. She paused every few seconds to discuss the situation with a burly man in a leather jacket. Only when Jake was a few feet away could he hear any of her hushed, staccato phrases.

'What happened, Benny? How did you end up in this place?'

Benny, for all his height and width, hung his head like a naughty schoolboy enduring a scolding. 'Mike said he wanted to visit some of the places he used to play when the band was just starting out. It seemed like a good idea at the time.'

She rolled her eyes. 'It always does, Benny.'

'Sorry, babe.'

She rolled her neck, as if she was trying to erase the kinks. 'So what happened, exactly?'

'Mike got to reminiscing with a couple of the locals. We were having a great time, buying everybody drinks and walking down memory lane, then some of the younger crowd got a bit mouthy and Mike flipped. He tried to thump one of them and tripped over a stool. They laughed, so he took another swing and hit the barman by accident.'

Benny shrugged. 'His aim is terrible after a few pints. He only knocked a tray of empties out of his hands—didn't hurt him.'

'Well, thank goodness for that!' She laid a hand on his arm. 'Listen, Benny, you see if you can get him upright, and I'll go and chat to the landlord. We need to get out of here before the press gets wind of it.'

The press? Jake thought. A pub brawl wasn't even going to make page sixteen of the local paper, let alone the nationals. Surely she was overreacting?

She stepped back to go and talk to the man behind the bar, giving him his first good look at the Porsche-driving god she had come to rescue. He couldn't have been more surprised. Mike wasn't some hot-looking young stud with a washboard stomach—he was a bedraggled-looking fifty-something with a beer belly. What on earth did she see in him?

He looked back at Serena, who was talking earnestly to the landlord. Frowns were giving way to nods and half-smiles. She marched back over to them, a less serious look on her face.

'He says he's not going to press charges. I've offered to pay for any damage, and a little bit extra for compensation. He seems quite happy, but I still think we ought to leave before he thinks better of it. Hand over the cash, Benny, and I'll sort this out right now.'

Benny handed her a wad of notes from his pocket.

Jake had the uncanny feeling this was not the first time she'd bailed the man out of trouble. It was almost as if she was on auto-pilot. Even so, she was marvellous. Nothing seemed to faze her.

Mike looked up at him. 'All right, mate?'

He held out his hand. Jake ignored it. The guy didn't seem to mind.

'She's great, isn't she?' he slurred, nodding his head towards Serena.

Jake resisted the urge to punch him.

'Yes, she is. You're very lucky she takes care of you like this.'

His head sagged. 'I know. She's the best daughter in the world.'

Daughter! Of course! He was so dense sometimes. He grinned to himself. Benny gave him an odd look, obviously wondering who the hell he was, and why he found the whole situation quite so funny.

Jake looked down at Serena's father again. Maybe his first impressions had been a little harsh, but jumping to conclusions about people was an everyday hazard when you had a runaway imagination like his. Mel was always quick to remind him of this fault. She said he needed to slow down and look at the facts, not just let his imagination fill in the blanks. He hated it when Mel was right.

Apart from being a little the worse for wear, Mike looked okay. In fact, he reminded Jake of someone. His forehead creased as he tried to find a match for the face in his memory bank. Nope, couldn't place it. It would come to him later. He was good with faces.

When they got outside, the clamping lorry was just disappearing round the corner with the Porsche strapped on board. All four of them stood and stared at the space where it had been parked.

'So much for a quick getaway,' mumbled Serena.

Jake was glad of the opportunity to be more than a spectator of the afternoon's increasingly bizarre turn of events. 'No problem. I can give you all a lift.'

Serena turned to look at him, as if she'd only just remembered he existed—a huge boost for the ego! Two hours ago he'd been having a rather nice lunch with the most fascinating woman he'd met in months, and now he'd been demoted to chauffeur and general onlooker. Oh, well, he might as well play the part.

'How about I drop Benny off at the car pound? I'll pay if you're short after forking out for damages in there—' he jerked his thumb in the direction of the pub '—and then we can get your dad home.'

She closed her eyes and breathed out through her nose. 'You know he's my dad?' she asked, without opening her eyelids.

'It came up.'

'Fabulous.'

Why was she so upset? It was hardly a matter of national security.

He put his arm round her shoulder and drew her to him. 'What do you say? Jump in the car and I'll take you somewhere warm. Let me return the favour and be your knight in shining armour for a change.'

To his amazement, she turned her face up to his and kissed his cheek. Her lips were warm and soft, and her hair smelled of lemons. When she moved away his cheek felt cold.

'You're a real gentleman, Charlie. Let's get going before anyone spots us.'

Benny wrestled Mike and his unruly limbs into the back seat, where he lolled against the door. Jake had the feeling he would have slithered onto the floor without the seat belt to hold him up. Serena took the passenger seat while Benny babysat Mike in the back.

No one talked as they sped back towards central London. They could hardly make polite chit-chat after the sort of afternoon they'd had. Even if they tried small talk, once they got past, *Isn't it getting dark in the evenings now?* or, *Very mild for November, isn't it?* they'd have lapsed back into the bottomless silence.

Jake turned the radio on low, to muffle the sound of Mike's snoring. He tuned it to an 'oldies-but-goldies' station. Nothing too offensive to anyone's tastes, he hoped. The opening chords of a song he hadn't heard for years drifted through the car. It reminded him of a summer on the housing estate when he and his mates had hung round the playground on their bikes. Before the see-saw had been vandalised. Before they'd started finding used syringes by the swings. He smiled and wondered what Martin and Keith were doing now.

Without warning, Mike burst from his coma and belted out the chorus of the song. He didn't have a bad voice. Jake glanced back just in time to catch a virtuoso air guitar performance.

That was it! He'd known he'd get it eventually.

Serena's dad looked like Michael Dove, the lead guitarist of Phoenix. This song had been one of their biggest sellers back in the late seventies. He breathed a sigh of relief. Not being able to place that face would have driven him mad all day.

He sneaked another look in the rear-view mirror. The resemblance was uncanny. This guy could make a good living as a look-alike, instead of getting wasted in dodgy south London pubs. Perhaps he should suggest it to Serena?

He looked again.

Yep, it was a great idea. Mike even had that same little scar on his lip…

'Jake!'

The flat of her hand hit him hard on the shoulder. Instinctively, he stamped on the brake pedal, suddenly noticing the brake lights of the car in front were a little too close for comfort. He forgot to put his foot back on the accelerator and looked into the back seat.

'You're Michael Dove.'

Serena groaned. He looked across at her. The car behind tooted its horn.

'You're Michael Dove's daughter.'

She looked back at him, her brows knit together.

'I know. Funnily enough, I have been all my life.'

Great! He was going to go all starry-eyed on her. Just when she'd thought she'd found a possible candidate for Mr Serendipity Dove.

Men responded in very different ways to the news that her

father was a rock legend, but the outcome was always the same. It was the kiss of death. Whether they pretended not to care, or decided to use the relationship to further their own careers, it changed things for ever.

She looked across at Jake. He was very quiet.

'But I thought Michael Dove's daughter was called something freaky, like Stardust or Moonbeam.'

A voice yelled from the back seat, 'Moonbeam, my—'

'Dad!'

'But Mr Three-piece-suit here thinks your name is ridiculous.'

Jake shook his head. 'There's nothing ridiculous about being called Serena. I was just saying—'

Serena groaned again. Which was not good. It was a seriously unattractive noise, but she couldn't stop herself. Earlier this afternoon she'd been a woman of mystery: exotic, alluring... Now Jake could find all the intimate details of her life just by picking up a tabloid newspaper.

'Who's Serena?' her dad muttered.

Jake leant across the gap between their seats and whispered, 'He must be in worse shape than he looks.'

I wish!

At least then her dad would pass out and save her from any further embarrassment. When she got home she was going to empty every bottle of spirits in their Chelsea townhouse down the kitchen sink. Including the one he kept in his guitar case he thought she didn't know about. And the whisky that was hidden in a wellington boot beside the back door.

Her father continued to mumble from the rear of the car, more to himself than for the benefit of the other passengers.

'Elaine named her...she was so thrilled—we thought we couldn't have kids. Then fortune smiled on us...'

If there was an ejector seat in Jake's BMW, she was praying fervently it would shoot her through the roof this very second.

'There's nothing wrong with Serendipity. It's a beautiful name. Moonbeam. I ask you…'

Jake coughed. 'I beg your pardon?'

'You heard!' she snapped.

There was a crinkle in his voice when he spoke next. She could tell he was holding back a snort of laughter, but, give him credit, he managed to arrest it by swallowing hard.

'It seems you were a little economical with your name, Miss Dove.'

'Yes, well, so were you, *Charles*!'

'Let's just call it quits and agree we are creatures of a similar nature.'

She allowed herself a small smile.

'Maybe.'

She turned to look at her father. He was fast asleep, mouth hanging open, threatening to dribble on Benny's shoulder if the car swung him in the right direction. Once again he was oblivious to the upheaval he'd created in her life. But it was hard to be cross with him. There was something so child-like about him. He didn't mean to cause trouble; he just couldn't help himself. It was as natural as breathing for him.

She closed her eyes and settled back into the comfy leather seat, letting the endless stopping and starting of the car journey lull her into a more relaxed frame of mind.

Later, after they'd bundled Dad into the house and up to his room, and Jake had made his excuses and left, she sat at the kitchen table with a steaming cup of tea between her hands and wondered if she'd ever see him again.

She thought perhaps not.

CHAPTER THREE

SERENA stared out across the London skyline in an effort to distract herself from the fact that very soon her bottom was going to be frozen to the wooden slats of the park bench. The bench's position on the brow of a hill offered little protection from the wind, even though it circled a towering sycamore.

'It's lovely here. What a view.'

Jake smiled and offered her a plate full of goodies from the picnic basket balancing between them. 'A favourite haunt of mine when I was younger.'

'Did you live close by?'

'Not too far.'

She could imagine him living in Blackheath, the exclusive area south of where they now sat in Greenwich Park. Blackheath itself was a mile-wide expanse of flat grass, its only vertical feature the razor-sharp spire of All Saints' church. Along the fringes of the heath were creamy Georgian villas, and she could easily imagine a young Jake bounding out of one of them each morning—grey shorts, school cap, laces undone.

'You can see it from here, actually,' he said.

She stared hard, but couldn't work out where he was pointing. The houses were too blurry and indistinct at this distance.

'You're looking in the wrong place.' He put an arm round

her shoulder and nudged her so she faced more to the west. 'You can't miss it. See the three tower blocks?'

'Beyond them?'

'No, *in* them. I used to live in the one on the far right. Four-teenth floor.'

She turned to look him in the eye. 'Really?'

'I could see this park from my bedroom window. A beautiful patch of green surrounded by pollution and concrete.'

She laughed. 'Very poetic.'

'Shh! You'll ruin my tough businessman image.'

'I'm not sure you're as tough as you look, Charlie.'

He gave her a sideways look. 'Why do you keep calling me that?'

'I don't know. It just seems to pop out of my mouth. It must suit you.'

His jaw hardened. 'I prefer Jake.'

'But it's not your real name.'

'Ah! So I get to use your given name as well, do I?'

'Good point. Jake it is.' She leaned back and looked up into the leafless branches above. 'Didn't you have a garden where you lived? Not even a shared one?'

She could hear him fiddling with the strap of the picnic basket. 'Do we have to do the childhood memories bit?'

'It's only fair. Even though I'm not famous myself, I'm related to someone who is, and that's good enough for the celebrity-hungry media. You could probably type my name into a search engine and find out what I had for breakfast last Wednesday.'

'I can think of better ways of finding out what you like for breakfast.' The edge in his voice was pure wickedness.

She rolled the back of her head against the tree trunk until she could see him. 'Nice try, but you're not going to throw me off track. I just want to know a little more about you. It's hardly a crime.'

'I normally get away with that kind of tactic.' He grinned, willing her to take the diversion he offered.

'I bet you do.'

His expression grew more serious. 'You're right. It's not a crime. I'm used to fluffing over the details my childhood. Some of my clients would faint if they thought a council estate yob was looking after their millions.'

Serena looked him up and down. How anyone could ever think of him as a yob was beyond her. Six-foot-something of pure elegance was standing right in front of her, from his cashmere coat to his hand-made shoes.

'There were hardly any trees on the estate, so I used to come here on the weekends—on days when the prospect of school was just too bleak.'

She picked up her plate—china, no less—and pinched a stuffed vine leaf between thumb and forefinger. Jake was staring at his old home, his eyes glazed with memories.

'I'd sit on this very bench and plot and plan my escape from the tower blocks. I'd watch the rest of the city going about its business and dream I could become a part of it one day.'

'Is that why you got into accounting?' She gave him a lazy smile. 'All that rabid excitement?'

'Ha, ha. Don't bother going down the all-accountants-are-boring route. I've heard all the jokes a million times. Anyway, at first I didn't want to be an accountant. I knew I needed money to get away from the estate, so I decided I'd better learn how to look after it properly. I got a job at a local accounting firm when I left school and it grew from there. Pretty soon I knew I'd found my niche, so I took the tests and worked hard until I qualified.'

'It sounds like you were very dedicated.'

'I wanted to get my mum away from there. She deserved something more than that.'

'I've heard those accounting exams are really difficult.'
She sighed. 'I've never stuck at anything like that. We were
always moving around too much. Dad was either on tour, or
recording in some far-flung place.'

'What did you do about school?'

'Well, up until I was eleven or so my mum home-schooled
me. My primary education was unconventional, to say the
very least. By the time I was ten I knew all about trees and
crystals and the constellations, but I was a little lacking in
the maths and science department.' She struck a pose. 'But I
was very good at improvisational dance and mime.'

Jake gave her another one of his heart-melting smiles.

'What happened after that?'

'Mum got ill and I was sent away to boarding school.'

His eyebrows lifted. 'I can't really see you in a starched
school uniform, having midnight feasts with Lady Cynthia.'

'If only! Have you heard of Foster's Educational Centre
in the West Country?'

He shook his head.

'One of the Sunday magazines did a feature on it a few
months ago—I thought you might have seen it. Anyway, it's
one of those so-called progressive schools, all fashionable
psychology and no common sense. Complete nuthouse, if
you ask me.' She winked at him. 'Needless to say, I didn't fit
in.'

'No! Of course not. The thought never crossed my mind.'

'Actually, I'm not joking. The other kids laughed at me
because they thought I was weird after my mum's special
brand of education. And, since the teachers believed that ex-
pressing negative energy was important to our emotional de-
velopment, it wasn't hard for the other kids to find ways to
torment me if they wanted to. Which they did. I was fresh
meat.'

'Ouch!'

'I left as soon as I could, and fled back to Dad. He'd just come out of rehab for his drug addiction. I'm assuming you know about that; it's pretty much common knowledge. He spent a few years living too fast and hard after my Mum died of cancer. He needed me home as much as I needed to get away.'

'What about a career?'

She snorted. 'Looking after Dad is a full-time job, believe me! I've been Dad's manager for the past five years. Consider me a personal assistant, troubleshooter and babysitter all rolled into one. The band don't do as much as they used to, but it can be pretty hectic at times.'

Jake handed her a glass of champagne. 'What would you do if you could do anything? Travel?'

She took a small sip and shook her head. 'No, not travel. My life has been nomadic enough. Something completely different.'

'Run away with the circus?'

She smiled at him and said nothing. It wouldn't do to reveal her real desires for the future. Announcing that your greatest wish was to become a wife and mother was like a starter's pistol for some men, and she wasn't ready to see this one disappearing in a cloud of dust.

Jake ticked all the right boxes: stable job, successful enough not to be after her dad's money, thoughtful, charming—the list was endless.

He put one hundred per cent commitment into all he did, and everything he did was first class. Just look at this hamper of picnic food from London's most exclusive department store. No ham sandwiches wrapped in an empty bread bag here.

But something inside her longed for ham sandwiches, lemonade, and children running down the hill with jam on their faces and grass stains on their knees.

She'd had enough champagne to fill a lifetime. It had lost its sparkle for her. Probably because she'd seen her father drink enough for two or three lifetimes. She'd been pushing him to get help for his drinking, and, although he denied it furiously, she thought he was almost ready to go back to rehab. The alternative didn't bear thinking about. Dad was the only family she'd got, and she was hanging onto him. Tight. Just entertaining any negative thoughts in that direction made her shudder.

'Cold?'

'A little.'

Jake put a protective arm round her and she leaned back on him. They said nothing more as they ate the last morsels of their picnic, but she took great care not to give Jake an opportunity to move away. The kind of heat he was generating had absolutely nothing to do with layers of jumpers and wool coats, and everything to do with the man inside them. If only she could hibernate like this, huddled up to him, until spring. It was wonderful to let someone else do the caring, just for a little bit.

When they had finished, Jake picked up the basket and offered a hand to help her up. Such a gentleman! He didn't release her hand when they started to walk down the path, and she didn't want him to. Even without the tickle of electricity that crept up her arm, the simple gesture of human contact felt good. It had been too long since she'd held hands with anyone.

They passed the Royal Observatory and took the little railed path that crossed the hill beneath it. Jake refused to release her hand as they negotiated the kissing gate there. It took quite a while before they untangled themselves enough to pass through. She had more than a sneaking suspicion that Jake had been deliberately clumsy with the hamper, just to keep them squashed up together while they swung the gate open in the confined space.

Once free of the gate, she was going to walk on, but Jake stopped moving and her arm tugged taut. She glanced back at him, puzzled.

He looked down at their feet and she followed suit. A brass strip was embedded in the tarmac, symbolising the point where the Greenwich meridian dissected not only the path, but the city. Jake hadn't crossed it, and they stood facing each other, as if at a threshold.

'Zero degrees longitude,' he said, looking deep into her eyes. 'A place of beginnings.'

If Jake thought today was only a beginning, it meant there was more to come. She couldn't stop her mouth from curling at the thought. 'Don't you think this is a bit surreal? We're standing so close, but we're in different hemispheres.'

'We're not *that* close.' He dropped the picnic basket by his side and took hold of her other hand. 'We could be closer.' In demonstration, he tugged her towards him so the fronts of their coats met and her eyes were level with his chin. She could feel his breath at her hairline. If she tipped her chin up just a notch his lips would be *so* close.

The heat of a blush stained her cheeks. No one had ever made her feel this way. The only point of contact was their fingers, yet her pulse galloped like a runaway horse.

'Still feeling strange?' he whispered into her hair.

'I think it's worse, if anything.' She swallowed hard, and raised her eyes to meet his. They were impossibly blue beneath his dark brows, and he wasn't smiling any longer. Deep in his eyes she saw a flicker of something previously hidden. Beneath the smooth-talking, city-slicker image, this was a good man, with a good heart.

His voice was warm on her cheek. 'A few more millimetres and we could really set the world spinning on its axis.'

'That was really cheesy,' she whispered back.

Still, it didn't stop her eyelids fluttering closed as his lips made the achingly slow journey to hers. In the moment just before they touched, she trembled uncontrollably.

It was everything a first kiss should be. Soft, sweet, full of promise. Never mind about separate hemispheres, they seemed to be the only two people on the planet. She clung to him and buried her fingers in his thick hair—the way she'd been longing to ever since their lives had collided in the rush hour traffic only a few days ago.

His palms cupped her face and his fingers stroked her jaw.

Never had she been kissed like this. It had never been anything more than a clashing of lips and teeth with the drifters she'd gone out with when she had been younger, and stupid enough to believe they could fill the empty spaces in her heart. Kissing Jake was so different. The sensation travelled from her lips right into her very soul.

Too soon he pulled away, tugged her crocheted hat a little more firmly onto her head, and led her down the path towards his car. All she could focus on for the rest of the afternoon was when—please, let it be *when*, not *if*—the next kiss was coming.

If Cassie had been any more desperate for information, she'd have been dribbling.

'I want to hear all the gory details.'

'I'm pretending I don't know what you're talking about, Cass. Absolutely nothing about my love-life could ever be described as "gory".'

'Not even the crash-and-burn flings of the past?'

'Yes…well… That was then—this is now.' She gave what she hoped was a superior look. 'I have evolved.'

Cassie grinned and shuffled a little closer. 'Come on, girl-friend. How's it going with the hot-shot accountant?'

'You know, Cass, a vicar's wife can definitely *not* pull off a word like "girlfriend".'

'Not even one with funky pink hair and a nose-stud?'

She smiled. Cassie was the most unconventional minister's wife you could hope to see. Her short baby pink hair stuck up every which way, and she had four holes in each ear and one in her nose. 'Not even close, darling.'

'Shame. I pick phrases like that up from the youth group. I hardly notice I'm doing it. Anyway, stop being the word police and tell me what I want to know. Resistance is futile. You should know that by now.'

'You never change, do you?'

'Not since that day I waltzed into the common room at Foster's and saved you from *another* year of sitting in the corner writing doleful little poems you wouldn't let anybody read.'

Serena gasped in horror. 'My poetry was never doleful! Rambling and self-indulgent, maybe, but never doleful.'

'Whatever. You needed a little livening up.'

'You certainly did that!'

'What did Prudence and her gang call us again?'

Serena clapped her hands and grinned. 'The freaky twins!'

'Joined at the hip for evermore!' yelled Cassie, punching the air.

'Until you met Steve, anyway. I should be cross, but he's such a sweetie I forgave you ten seconds after I met him.'

Cassie stared off into space and her streetwise demeanour melted. 'He is rather wonderful…'

'Do you remember what your parents said when you told them about him?'

'Do I? They totally freaked! I can still hear my father—' She dropped her voice an octave to a low rumble. 'Cassandra. You're only nineteen. You're far too young to understand what marrying into the *establishment* means.'

They both collapsed in a heap of giggles.

Serena sighed and wiped a finger under her eye. 'At least

they came round in the end. They practically fall over themselves now to tell their friends that their son-in-law runs an inner city project for underprivileged kids.'

'Ah, yes, but the dog collar still makes them squirm.'

'And you love it.'

Cassie giggled into her coffee mug.

'You're a minx, Cassie Morton.'

'It's why you love me.'

'No, I love you because you're the best friend anyone could ever have.' All traces of laughter left her voice and she fixed Cassie with a solemn stare. 'You're right. You *did* save me that last year at Foster's. It would have been hell without you. I owe you big-time.'

Cassie's eyes sparkled. 'And I know a way you can repay me.'

Serena slumped on the kitchen table in defeat. 'Go on. Pass me the carrot cake, and I'll tell you everything.'

Cassie just smiled, cut a thick wedge of cake, and plopped it on a chipped willow pattern plate. Serena dragged it across the table towards her, dipped her finger in the cream cheese icing and tried to think of where to start.

She almost didn't want to share this with Cass, which was a first. Not that she thought she would jinx it if she talked about Jake, but because it all seemed too precious. She wanted to keep all the memories locked up inside her. She'd have to tell Cass something, though, or she'd get the thumb-screws out.

'He's definitely in the running for Mr Right. We've had dinners and picnics and been to the ballet. I always thought there was more to a date than standing in the back of a smoky pub watching my other half play pool. It's like being Cinderella…'

'You've got it bad!'

She stared at the carrot cake, but didn't take a bite, her

appetite arrested by the thoughts swirling round her head. 'Do you think so? Is this what *really* falling in love feels like?'

'Well, that depends. How do you feel?'

She sighed. 'He's all I can think about. When I'm not with him I've got butterflies thinking about the next time we'll meet, and when we're together I get butterflies just because I'm with him! He makes me feel special. For the first time I think I've met a man who likes *me*. Not Michael Dove's daughter, but me.'

Cassie put her coffee down and cocked her head on one side.

'So, have you…?'

'Have I what?'

'You know.'

She took a large bite of cake and shook her head. Chewing and swallowing was a great way to stall, but regrettably her mouth was soon free again. 'You know I vowed it would take a ring on my finger as a guarantee of intentions before…that. I've been foolish too many times in the past where men are concerned. My creep-radar is completely defunct.'

Cassie nodded. 'I know. Every loser carrying a guitar pick was *the one*.'

'You'd think I'd know better, wouldn't you? I mean, I've been around musicians all my life. I know exactly how reliable they are. But there's something about arty types I can't resist. I've tried to fight it, but every time I end up getting hit with a sucker-punch and I'm totally gone.'

'Knocked out and down for the count. It's never pretty,' said Cassie, screwing up her face.

Serena rested her chin on her hand and stared out of the window. 'I've tried to analyse it. It just doesn't make sense. The best I've come up with is that it's something to do with those wild imaginations that make every day a surprise, that passion for life—'

'The attention span of a gnat,' added Cassie, finishing with a huge bite of cake.

'You're so right. And that's why I've sworn off men like that.'

Cassie mumbled through a mouthful of crumbs. 'And why I'm doing the vetting from now on.'

Serena sat back in her chair and wondered if the reason she fell so hard and fast was simpler than she allowed herself to believe. Maybe her childhood had left her so desperate for someone to love that she grabbed anything that vaguely resembled the real thing with both hands. Of course it was invariably a mirage—looked good at the time, but ultimately left her feeling dry and unsatisfied.

That was why she was pacing herself this time, taking it slow. Jake was different from anybody else she'd been out with, but it was still early days. She wanted him to be *the one*, but it was too early to tell.

She took another bite of cake. The ever-present butterflies did a little waltz as she imagined the fireworks that could happen once 'Prince Charming' had been well and truly stamped on Jake's forehead.

Jake couldn't walk past the painting without having a third go at getting it straight. He nudged the left corner a little. There. He took three steps back and tipped his head slightly.

Blast! It had looked better before he'd started messing around with it.

It was just that he wanted everything right. Tonight he was cooking Serena dinner, playing on home turf—a departure from his normal routine. Now he had the money to enjoy such luxuries, he liked to wine and dine his girlfriends at good restaurants. They seemed to appreciate it too.

The perfectionist side of his nature urged him to pull out all the stops when he took a woman out, and his competitive spirit made him want to do that little bit better than the next guy. Even if his relationships didn't last, he wanted his old flames to remember him as the perfect gentleman. It was a little vain, perhaps, but he liked to think at least one or two of his ex-girlfriends thought of him occasionally and let out a little *if only* sigh.

He lifted his hand to tap the frame again, but pulled it back before it made contact. What was wrong with him? He wasn't usually this jumpy before a date. Perhaps it was because Serena was so totally different from the type of woman he was normally attracted to.

Ever since he'd had hormones in enough quantities to notice girls, he'd pined after cool, sophisticated types. Like the girls from St Bernadette's, the exclusive private school only a mile or so from Ellwood Green.

It had never seemed odd to him that such a bastion of old money was so close to his home. The school had probably been built for the daughters of wealthy merchants when Deptford had been a bustling port. Now the docks were miles downstream, and Deptford was no longer the prosperous suburb it had once been, but the evidence was still visible if you walked the streets. You could be walking past boarded-up shops one minute and down leafy roads with ornate Victorian masonry the next. Little pockets of poverty and privilege, side by side, but worlds apart. London was like that.

He smiled. The girls from St B's had looked so good in their crisp white blouses and pleated skirts. He'd bet they'd smelled good too. Not that they'd let a grubby little oik like him close enough to find out. Perversely, the way they'd lifted their noses when they passed him in the street had only made him want them more. Probably because they represented everything he'd ever craved—class, style, money—although he hadn't analysed that feeling at the time.

Then, one day, when he hadn't reeked of the council estate any longer, the snooty noses had lowered and they'd given him sidelong glances from beneath their lashes.

How stupid of him not to have seen it before. He'd been dating St Bernadette's girls in one shape or form ever since he'd owned his first Rolex. Except Chantelle. She was the one exception—and his biggest mistake.

He glanced down at his watch. Scratches marred the surface in a few places, but he would never replace it. He'd saved every penny he could from his first pay packets at Jones and Carrbrothers until he could strut into the jewellers and slap down a wad of cash for it. It had been an important symbol. One that shouted, *I've made it*!

Once it had been paid for, he'd rented a shoebox bedsit and started the process of erasing his past—from the chain-store clothes to the flat vowels of his cockney accent. Nobody who met him now would ever suspect. He took great pains to ensure his rich clients would never guess their family money was being looked after by the son of a petty criminal.

He'd surprised himself by telling Serena his history. Okay, he'd left out some pretty major details, but he'd also let slip more than he usually did. Somehow it didn't matter if she knew. She wasn't impressed by his money in the slightest, which, after the initial dent to his ego, had been a huge relief. He was tired of women who earmarked him as a *good prospect*.

But it was more than that. Despite all their differences, they had a common bond. She knew what it was like to be an outsider too.

He walked out into the hall and headed back to the kitchen. The sight of the crease-free bedcovers through the bedroom door made his insides clench. An image flashed in his mind: he was standing holding a tray while morning sun filtered through the curtains onto a tangle of arms and legs in the duvet. Dark, silky hair sprawled on the pillow.

Abruptly, he reached for the doorknob and pulled the door shut. He had to get a hold of himself. Rushing ahead was definitely not the way to go with Serena.

He was courting her. It was an old-fashioned idea, but it fitted, nevertheless—and it was delicious. A tantalising game. They circled round each other, prolonging the inevitable, but the circles were getting smaller and smaller. Sooner or later there would be an explosive impact.

He would just have to keep himself on a tight leash until then. But that should be no problem. He was used to keeping control when it came to relationships. Women in his past had tried to push and prod him into doing what they wanted, but he'd always remained firmly anchored. He called the shots. He took the lead in pursuing his quarry at the start of the relationship, and he always decided when it was time to end it—normally the instant he saw the glitter of diamond rings in her eyes.

Mel said he was heartless, but he told himself it was for his ex-girlfriends' protection. There was no point giving them hope of a happy-ever-after. It wasn't in his genes.

Just as well he didn't have to worry about all that with Serena. Her heritage was flower-power and free love. As she'd said on their first date, they didn't need to tie themselves down. They could take the relationship one day at a time and see where it took them, which was great. He felt freer to be himself if he didn't have to worry about her getting the wrong idea.

He reached the kitchen and hunted for the corkscrew so he could open a bottle of Pinot Noir. He'd just pulled it out of the drawer when the telephone whined.

Please don't let this be Serena, ringing to cancel!

'Hello?'

'Hi, big brother.' Mel was trying to be chirpy.

'What's up?'

There was a pause and a heartfelt sigh.

'Mel?'

'It's Dad.'

Jake's back straightened. 'What about him?'

'There've been a few sightings lately.'

'On the Costa Blanca?'

'No, not in Spain—here.'

Jake marched across the kitchen and yanked the fridge door open, although when the blast of cold air hit his face he had no idea what he'd come to fetch, if anything. 'I've told you before. I don't care what that man does, as long as he doesn't come within fifty feet of me.'

'It's been ten years. Aren't you even curious?'

'No. He won't have changed. Don't fall for his flannel, Mel.'

Her tone was defensive. 'What makes you think I'm going to see him?'

'I didn't say you were. Are you?'

Silence.

'You were much younger than me when he left. You don't remember half of what went on—and there was lots of stuff I made sure you didn't find out. I know you've got these fairy-tale ideas that he'll come back and it'll be happy families, but it's not going to happen, Mel. He'll pick your pocket the same time as giving you a hug.'

Her voice was quiet. He knew she was on the verge of tears, but he wasn't prepared to have her hurt. He had to be tough with her now to stop worse pain in the future. All the same, he didn't want to unleash the anger reserved for his father on Mel.

He softened his voice. 'I'm sorry, sis, that's just the way it is.'

'I know. I just wish it wasn't, you know?' She sniffed. 'I thought I should tell you, that's all.'

'Thanks. I'm glad you did.'

Another sniff. 'Well, I'd better be getting on…'

'Take care of yourself. I'll see you on Sunday, okay? Don't cry for him, Mel. He's not worth it.'

'I'll try. Bye, Jake.' There was a gentle but despondent click as she put the receiver down.

Jake resisted flinging his phone against the dark slate tiles of the kitchen floor and carefully placed it back in its cradle. Hadn't that man done enough damage in the past? Why couldn't he have just stayed *disappeared*? He wrenched the door of the glass cabinet open. He'd bet last year's salary that the reason for Charlie Jacobs's return was not a good one.

CHAPTER FOUR

JAKE walked back towards the bottle of wine. Grinding the corkscrew into the cork felt good. Just the scent of chocolate and cherries as he poured it into a goblet eased the creases from his forehead. The doorbell chimed.

He walked into the hallway, glass in hand, and checked the screen of the video entry system. The camera looked down upon a head of dark, glossy hair. She was fiddling with her nails. Suddenly she turned and stared straight at the camera.

He actually jumped back slightly, almost as if he'd been caught spying. She gave the camera a saucy wink. It took him a good few seconds before he remembered to press the button, and the buzzer sounded long after she'd disappeared inside.

He swung his front door open and waited for her, heart thumping.

Calm. Calm.

Never lose your cool in front of a woman, remember? Who was he kidding? His cool had run screaming from the room the first time he'd laid eyes on Serena, and he hadn't found its hiding place yet. Still, better not to let *her* know that.

He held the glass out to her as she rounded the corner. 'Perfect timing.'

She took it and glided past him into the flat. 'That's what I like,' she said, and stopped to take a sip. 'A man who knows what I need even before I do.'

Jake took a little bow.

A naughty grin spread across her face. 'I'm getting a little 1950s flashback here. Shouldn't I be saying, *Hi, honey. I'm home?*'

'Not if you don't actually live here.'

She ignored him and waved the glass in his direction. 'By rights, *this* should really be a martini and you—' A finger lifted from the stem of her glass and jabbed the air. '*You* ought to be wearing a frilly apron.'

That was what he liked about her. She was always seeing things from a different angle. He pulled her close and kissed her ever so gently on the lips. When they pulled apart she whispered in his ear. 'Actually, I think you'll do quite nicely just as you are.'

He took her by the hand and led her into the kitchen.

'Dinner smells nice. Where did you order from?'

'*Chez Jake.* Do you know it?'

'I'm not falling for that one! Don't you know that's trick number five in the bachelor handbook on how to impress women? Order a good takeaway and pass it off as your own. And if I'm not mistaken…' She edged over to the bin and popped the lid up with a flourish of her hands. 'Ta-dah!'

The smug smile evaporated from her face as she looked down into the carton-free bin. Her eyebrows rose. 'You mean you actually cooked it all by yourself? I *am* impressed!'

'You haven't tasted it yet.'

'But you really cooked? For me?'

'Yes, I really did.'

A softness glittered in her eyes and she took a quick sip of her wine. When she looked up again it was gone.

He stirred the bubbling sauce. 'Would you take the wine

and the glasses through to the dining room for me? It's just opposite.'

Serena hesitated, then walked over and gave him a feather-light peck on the cheek.

'Thank you, Jake.'

He stopped stirring and frowned. Thank you for what? It was only dinner.

Serena placed the glasses on coasters and surveyed the bone china plates, silver cutlery and elegant wine flutes that were laid ready on the table. Long-stemmed candlesticks flanked an arrangement of fresh flowers in the centre. Never in her wildest dreams had she imagined a man would pamper her so. Jake must be *really* serious about her. The ramifications of that thought made her heart skip a little faster.

The most she'd ever got from a boyfriend before was a packet of peanuts thrown across the pub table after he'd been to the bar. In her experience, musicians who knew she had a rich father didn't bother frittering their hard-earned cash on her—quite the opposite. But it wasn't the quality of Jake's chinaware that impressed her. It had taken time and careful thought to create all this—just for her. It was utterly seductive.

Jake called from the kitchen. 'Sit yourself down. I'll be there in just a sec.'

She pulled out a chair and did as she was told, still marvelling at his domesticity. A vase full of creamy white roses sat in front of her. They were lovely, buds loosening with the promise of the fullness. Just like the perfect blooms of a bridal bouquet.

Clinking dishes announced Jake's arrival. She was about to compliment him on the table setting, but all she could do when she looked up was hoot with laughter. Over the top of his jeans and shirt he was wearing the most hideous floral apron she had ever seen. Jake just grinned back at her, not fazed at all by the combination of psychedelic blue flowers and designer shirt.

He set the starters down on the table while she wiped her eyes, trying hard to leave her mascara intact. It took quite a while before the end of her sentences weren't hi-jacked by a burst of giggles.

'Where the heck did you dig that up?'

Jake did a twirl. 'You don't think it suits me?'

'Oh, beautifully! In fact, I think you should wear it next time we go out.'

'How about next Thursday? At your special birthday dinner?'

She gasped. 'How did you know it was my birthday next week?'

'A handy little tool called a search engine.'

He'd been looking her up on the internet? If anyone else had said that she'd have found it creepy—definite boyfriend marching orders! But she already knew Jake wasn't like that. Anyway, it would be highly hypocritical of her to be cross. Hadn't she visited his firm's website nearly every day, just to look at the pixellated little photo of him and convince herself he wasn't some longed-for figment of her imagination? She was secretly flattered he'd done something similar.

She tried not to look too gooey as she smiled back at him. 'So, where are you taking me?'

Jake put a finger to his lips. 'It's a surprise. But I promise you this: it's going to be a night you'll never forget.'

She hastily studied the goats' cheese salad in front of her. 'You're too good to me.'

He sounded shocked. 'I thought you'd be used to getting the princess treatment. I can't believe no one has ever looked into those big brown eyes and said you deserve the best.'

She swallowed a little lump that clogged her throat. 'Mum did. But that was a long time ago—a different life, almost. She died when I was twelve.'

He took her hand and she looked up into his bottomless blue eyes, so full of compassion. Suddenly it didn't matter if he saw that hers were tear-filled. He saw parts of her that other men hadn't even noticed, let alone understood. It was as if she was transparent to him. Yet she didn't feel naked or scared, she just felt *known*.

He pulled her hand towards his lips and placed the tiniest kiss on her knuckle. Nothing to prepare her for the shock-wave that shot up her arm and bullseyed in her heart.

Her breath caught in her throat as he said, 'I'm going to have to do a lot of making up for lost time, then.'

Dinner was fantastic. The conversation was warm and intimate. If a world existed outside the candlelit cocoon they shared, she didn't want to know about it. She swallowed the last bite of her seafood pasta and relaxed back into her chair.

'That was amazing!' The corners of her mouth curled up. 'You could take the apron off now, if you wanted to.'

His eyes jerked downwards, then he laughed. 'I completely forgot I was wearing it!' He tugged at the ties behind his back and slipped it over his head.

'So where did you get it? I'm going to be very scared if I find out you have a row of them hanging in your wardrobe!'

'No, you're safe. This belongs to my cleaning lady. She keeps it in the hall cupboard with her cleaning supplies. You don't think a single guy living alone is this good at dusting, do you?' He bunched the apron up and slung it under his arm. 'I'd better put this back. Do you want coffee?'

'Please.'

Serena busied herself with collecting the plates and

followed Jake down the hall. So he didn't dust—who cared? Neither did she. But in every other way Jake was shaping up to be Mr Perfect.

By the time she'd wandered into the kitchen, Jake was pouring steaming espresso into delicate little cups. He took the dishes from her hands, passed her a coffee, then laced his fingers in her spare hand and tugged her towards the living room. 'We'll leave the washing up for now.'

'Fine by me.' Her eye was immediately drawn to the tall windows that almost filled one side of the room. 'Oh, wow! You've got a balcony! I've always wanted a balcony.'

'There's not much to see. In a densely populated area like this, it's just gardens and back windows.'

'Can I take a look?'

'Knock yourself out.'

She put down her coffee cup, unfastened the brass catch, and stepped through the French windows onto a narrow wrought-iron balcony. She could have spent an hour out there, listening to the shuffle of the wind in the trees and nosing into the uncurtained windows.

Jake's presence was noticeable more from the heat of his body behind hers than the sound of his footsteps. He draped his arms around her shoulders like a knotted pullover and she sank back into him.

'If I lived in this flat, I'd spend all my time out here.'

'Would you? I like the trees, but it's a bit too crowded. Still, it'll do until I've saved up for my house in the country.'

'Don't you think it looks magical? Especially now people are starting to put their Christmas lights up.'

Jake grunted. 'It's only the second week of December! Far too early for all that stuff.'

'So that's why your place is twinkle-free, is it?'

'I don't *do* Christmas lights.'

Serena thought of the dog-eared tinsel and her mother's

hand-made decorations that graced the nine-foot tree in her living room. 'Shut up, you old humbug, and give me a kiss!'

She swivelled to face him and their lips met. All she was conscious of for the next few seconds was the heady mixture of Jake's lips on hers and the heat trapped between their torsos. Even after three weeks, his kisses had the power to reduce her nerve-endings to frazzles. If anything, there was a cumulative effect. It seemed impossible that each kiss could be sweeter than the last, but Jake was doing his best to give her solid empirical proof.

The mood shifted. What had started out as romantic and sensual was rapidly intensifying into something else entirely. Her guard was too far down. It was all she could do to lock her knees and keep herself from puddling to the floor. Jake's hand was under her jumper, caressing her midriff and snaking a tantalising journey up her body.

A tiny voice screeched at her from the back of her head, telling her it was too soon, too intense. She'd promised herself, no matter what, that she'd use her brain rather than her hormones to set the pace. If Jake really liked her, he'd wait...

Trembling, she let the cold air rush between their lips and slid round in the circle of his arms to face outwards again. Her heart stamped an angry beat in her chest and she took a few deep, cleansing breaths.

She closed her hands over the top of his, if only to stop the mesmerising rhythm of his fingers as he stroked her bare flesh. The slice of December wind against her face was a welcome jolt. Nearly as good as a cold shower.

However, Jake didn't seem to notice it. He nuzzled into the side of her neck and placed tiny kisses along her jaw. She had to do something to break the spell, so she straightened a little and ordered herself to pay attention to the view.

'Isn't it fascinating—looking into all the windows, watching other people go about their lives?'

Jake clasped her even closer, his breath raising the sensitive hairs inside her ears.

'Riveting.'

She struggled to ignore the exquisite tickle of his lips on her earlobe. She was pretty sure if anyone took an X-ray of her insides right now, they'd be staring at a quivering mass of strawberry jelly.

She picked a window and focused intently on a mother pacing a repetitive circuit with a tiny baby propped on her shoulder. Although the pane muffled any sound, she could tell by the infant's red scrumpled face that it was not in a happy place. Every few seconds they disappeared as the woman changed direction, but she always reappeared in the same place.

The hypnotic quality of her movements was certainly working on Serena, who suddenly noticed Jake's hands had worked free of hers. The combination of lips and fingertips was fatal. Her eyes slid closed and her lips parted. A tiny intake of breath that sounded very much like an *ah* brought her to her senses slightly.

Focus, girl. *Focus.*

She wrenched her eyelids open and searched for another window. Two floors down, she found one. A couple—married, probably—pottered around their kitchen. He stirred a pot; she opened a bottle of wine. They were so unhurried, hardly making eye contact, but they moved around each other in a well-choreographed sequence they must have practised a thousand times, opening drawers and cupboards, dishing up their meal. She couldn't tear her eyes away. Even the movement of Jake's lips against her skin was almost forgotten as she watched them circling round each other in their seemingly mundane dance.

In the pit of her stomach, she ached for just a little of what they had.

'It's freezing out here, Jake. Let's go back inside.'

He made no fuss, only smiled at her and opened the door for her to step through. Once inside, he fastened the catch and closed the curtains, so not a chink of the outside world remained visible.

But in her imagination she could still see the couple, sitting at a little square table, swapping stories from their day at work. She gave him an easy smile, sweet with promise. He touched her hand as she reached for her glass…

Serena tried to erase the image by taking an active interest in her surroundings. Jake's furniture was expensive. Classic designs with a modern twist. She could have opened the pages of any one of the aspirational interior design magazines at the supermarket and seen something identical. Almost.

As she looked more closely, she noticed elements that jarred. There were too many books for a truly minimalist look—and not just work-related tomes. Novels, poetry and biographies jostled for position on the cluttered shelves. Colourful modern art canvases hung on the walls. She would have expected abstract designs in beige and brown, not Kandinsky and Chagall. In the corner, a glossy acoustic guitar with a ratty strap was propped up against a small table.

'Do you play?' she asked, nodding towards it.

'I used to.'

'Not any more?'

'Well…I pick it up now and again. I'm very rusty. I just don't have the time.'

'Play me something.'

Jake shifted in his seat. Ridges appeared on his forehead. 'You don't want to hear me twanging away after listening to your old man. I wouldn't compare favourably.'

'Pass it here, then.'

'Yes, Miss.'

She sat the guitar on her lap and, one at a time, pressed

the fingers of her left hand onto the strings. It took all her concentration to strum the few bars of the only song she knew. It was about as comfortable and familiar as bungee jumping. She stopped mid-verse and looked at Jake. His eyebrows were hitched halfway up to his hairline.

'That has to be the worst rendition of "Scarborough Fair" I've ever heard.'

She bowed slightly in acknowledgement. 'The musical gene obviously took one look at me and decided to leap-frog a generation.'

'Not a carbon-copy of your father, then?'

'I don't think you'd find me half as attractive if I was.'

He laughed. 'You're right there!'

She clapped a decisive hand against the front of the guitar. 'Anyway, my point is this: anything you produce can only be a step up from my paltry efforts.'

He thrust out a hand. 'I don't think I can resist you in anything.'

She passed him the guitar and settled back into the sofa as he reprised the song she'd just butchered.

'You're good,' she said, when he had finished a verse and a chorus.

'I'll take that as a compliment, from a woman who knows what good guitar sounds like even if she can't reproduce it.'

'Did you ever think of taking it further?'

'A career, you mean?'

'I suppose.'

'Not really. I needed to be sure I could earn a living so I could get Mum and Mel off the estate. Accountancy won out over music in that respect, no question.'

'Do you ever wish you'd had another choice?'

He shook his head. 'My life is exactly what I planned it would be. I wouldn't change a thing.'

His answer made her heart sink a little. She knew she

wanted safe and predictable in her future husband, but a wayward part of her still hankered after the creativity and verve of an artistic temperament.

Yes, and look where that has got you in the past! Stomped on, taken for granted and broken-hearted. Don't even go there!

While she had been arguing with herself, Jake had started strumming the guitar again. He was staring into space, not even watching his hands, yet they seemed to remember the chords of the haunting tune he played all on their own. She closed her eyes and let the gentle thrumming wash over her, until it petered out a few minutes later.

'That was beautiful. What was it?'

'Just something I wrote when I was younger. I've messed around with it for years, but I can never seem to find the right way to finish it.' He shrugged and slipped the guitar over the edge of his chair to rest against the bookcase. 'Guess I never will.'

'Don't stop. It's very relaxing.'

He swung the guitar back onto his lap and started picking away at the strings. She sipped her coffee and watched him lose himself in the rise and fall of the melody his fingers were weaving. He looked different while he was absorbed like that. Less polished, more vulnerable. A tingling feeling flared inside her as she realised she was seeing a side to Jake he normally kept well camouflaged. An imaginative, creative side that was totally at odds with the conservative suits and accounts ledgers.

Then it hit her like a kick in the stomach. This accountant had the soul of a musician!

It was at that exact moment Serendipity felt the familiar slap of a right hook out of nowhere.

'Jake, I'm scared! I don't know where we are!'

'All will be revealed shortly.'

She liked surprises as much as the next girl, but being dragged round half of London with a woolly scarf covering her eyes was too much. Jake had insisted on securing it round her head while they were in the taxi he'd hailed outside the restaurant. As if dinner at a Moroccan restaurant, sitting on cushions and feeling pampered and exotic, hadn't been enough, Jake now had something else up his sleeve. Something she was starting to wish would stay tucked up there.

She prised her fingers from the metal railing and let him guide her down a never-ending flight of stone stairs. It took all her resolve not to grab the rail and hang on for dear life. Every other step she felt she was falling, but Jake's warm strong hand was there, steadying her, making her feel safe.

Finally her feet reached a large, blessedly flat area. 'Can I take this off now?'

Jake's hand swatted her fingers away from the knot behind her head. 'Not yet.'

The scent of his aftershave clung to the fibres of the scarf, overloading her nostrils. It was as if he was wrapped around her. Apart from the odd twinkle of what she presumed to be streetlights through the weave, she could see nothing. The gentle slap of waves against stone told her they were somewhere near the river—probably the Thames embankment.

Jake's arm circled her waist and he propelled her forwards into the unnerving clatter of footsteps that swirled around them. Wherever they were, it was busy. After a minute or so, he came to a halt.

'Wait there. I'll only be a couple of steps away.'

'No! Don't let go!'

'You'll be perfectly safe. I just need to have a word with this young man over here.'

She clutched onto him with her gloved hand, but he pulled away gently.

'Trust me. I'll be with you in less than a minute.'

She heard him take a few steps, and his murmured voice mixed with another. She shuffled slightly in his direction and bumped into someone.

'Sorry!' she exclaimed, not even knowing whether she was talking to the person she'd barged into. She didn't dare move again, so she just stood there, letting the crowds eddy past her.

His arm enclosed her again. 'This way.'

The hard stone beneath her heels gave way to a clanging metal ramp. Where on earth were they? Soon they came to a stop. Jake steered her to face a certain direction.

'Now, Serena, it is very important that when I say *go*, you take a big step forwards. Okay?'

She nodded, suddenly feeling as if she was about to walk the plank. The lapping of water was louder, almost beneath her feet.

'Ready...?' She clenched her elbows to her sides, palms raised in front of her to ward off the danger she couldn't see.

'Go!'

She clamped her already blindfolded eyes shut and took the biggest step she could—feeling it was more a leap of faith—then clung on to Jake for all she was worth.

'We're moving!' she squeaked, then gripped him even tighter as she realised they weren't just moving sideways, they were climbing upwards too!

Jake just laughed softly, and kissed her forehead.

'Happy Birthday, Serena.' He prised his arms from her grasp, gently freed the knot in the scarf and pushed it back over her head.

'You can open them now. It's perfectly safe.'

She parted her eyelashes slowly, dazzled by the twinkling lights all around her. They were inside something. Her eyes just could not make sense of what she was seeing. Images jumbled into her brain. Lights...metal...glass. Then it all fell into place...

'We're on the London Eye!'

'You said you'd always wanted to go on it that day we had lunch at Maison Blanc.'

'How sweet of you to remember!'

She fell silent and took a good look around her. They were alone inside one of the egg-shaped glass and metal pods on the giant wheel almost directly across the Thames from the Houses of Parliament. She'd never seen London look so beautiful. It hardly felt as if they were moving, but slowly they were climbing into the night sky. A whole city of Christmas lights below twinkled just for them. She pressed her nose against the glass and stared.

The unmistakable pop and hiss of a champagne cork made her turn round. He was smiling that wonderful, heart-melting smile of his, and pouring champagne into a pair of glasses that seemed to have appeared from nowhere, along with an ice-bucket.

'How did you do all this?'

'It took a little bit of planning, but it wasn't impossible. I told you we had a little catching up to do to make you feel special.'

'I think you've done it all in one night!'

'What makes you think this is all there is?'

'There's more?'

'You haven't had your present yet.'

She looked past him to the ice-bucket. No brightly wrapped parcel stood beside it. She bent down and looked under the oval-shaped wooden bench in the centre of the pod. Nothing.

'So where is it? No, don't tell me—you're having it heli-coptered in when we get a little higher?'

He laughed and patted the breast pocket of his jacket. 'It's right here, but I was going to wait until we got to the top to give it to you.'

Serena swallowed. It was getting hard to think.

Her present was obviously very special. After all, he was making the act of giving it to her a monumental occasion.

And it was small enough to fit into his pocket.

It couldn't be…could it?

No. That was a stupid idea! It was far too soon.

Jake handed her a glass of champagne and stood beside her to survey the patchwork of the London skyline. They sipped in silence as the pod climbed higher, but she couldn't concentrate on the illuminations on Battersea Bridge, or St Paul's Cathedral. All she could think about was what might be sparkling inside his suit pocket.

It seemed as if the wheel had gone into slow motion. It took a torturously long time for their pod to reach the apex. Just as they watched the one above theirs start to descend, Jake turned towards her and looked deep into her eyes. The entire herd of butterflies resident in her stomach stampeded and came to settle, fluttering madly, in her chest.

'I want you to know you are the most fascinating woman I've ever met…'

Her mouth went dry.

'I don't think anyone has had the effect on me that you do. And, because of that, I want to give you something that is uniquely for you—something I've never given to anybody else.'

Her eyes followed his right hand as it slipped inside his jacket and reached into the pocket that covered his heart. When it reappeared, it was holding a small, velvet-covered jewellery box. Square. Ring-sized.

One hand flew to her mouth and she clutched the glass of champagne as if it were a lifeline. She was no longer aware of the motion of the giant wheel. It seemed to have stopped on her in-breath. The world paused as they floated high above a sea of sparkling diamonds.

He faced the box towards her and gently eased the lid open, to reveal the most wonderful…

CHAPTER FIVE

EARRINGS?

She looked up at him. His eyes held a question.

She checked the box again, just to make sure she was seeing straight.

No, she was right. It was definitely a pair of silver earrings sitting on the velvet cushion. Actually, they were the most exquisite design of interwoven ivy, completely unlike anything she'd ever seen before. They were really...*her*. They just weren't...

She ignored the fact that her stomach had plummeted from where they were suspended mid-air to the slime-coated riverbed below, and choked out the only words that came to mind.

'They're...earrings.'

Jake frowned. He almost let that mask of his slip. Just for a split-second he looked really vulnerable. 'You don't like them?' He shook his head slightly. 'I was sure the designer's work was just your taste, but—'

'No, Jake. They're amazing. Really.'

He searched her face.

'Then why do you look as if you're just about to cry?'

She set her glass down on the bench, took his head in her hands and kissed away his frown. When she thought she'd stopped shaking enough to sound convincing, she pulled away.

'Jake. The earrings are stunning. Nobody has ever given me a present that suited me so well. In fact, they don't just suit me, they sum me up.' And she didn't have to lie. They were perfect. He'd obviously had them made just for her. 'I'm just crying because I'm so…happy.'

The first of a hundred tears was poised and ready at the corner of her eye. She hugged him hard as it escaped down her cheek and screwed her face up against his shoulder, willing the other ninety-nine to stay put.

'Let me put them in for you.'

She moved back enough to remove the hoops she already wore, and dropped them in her coat pocket. Jake took one of the delicate earrings from the box between his fingers and aimed for the hole in her earlobe.

'Ow!' The spike of the earring stabbed tender flesh.

'I'm hurting you.'

'No. Well, a little. Maybe I'm better off on my own.' She forced the corners of her mouth upwards. 'Why don't you get me a refill?'

By the time he'd returned, with a full glass of champagne, both earrings were securely fastened in place.

'You're sure you like them?'

She pressed a delicate kiss onto his cheek. 'I love them.' *I love you.*

'Well…okay. Good.'

They spent the last ten minutes of the ride in silence. He seemed a little distant. She hoped desperately that he hadn't caught her awkward stutter when she'd opened the box. It didn't matter that the little velvet cube hadn't contained what her over-active imagination had conjured up. They'd been seeing each other less than a month. It had been crazy to think…

She would probably laugh about it in the morning when she spoke to Cass on the phone.

The pod reached the landing and the doors whooshed open. Back into the real world. Dirt, noise, pollution. Nothing like the fairytale scene from the top of the wheel at all, really.

Jake stood in front of the black-painted door and waited for the chime of the doorbell to fade. Part of him wished she wasn't there, that the door would stay shut.

'Hey! Up here.'

He squinted and looked up. Serena was leaning out of a first-floor window, looking extraordinarily beautiful, with her dark hair falling forwards and a huge smile on her face. She was so pleased to see him. He felt like an utter heel.

She pointed to a narrow passageway at the side of the enormous Chelsea townhouse. 'Come round to the back door. I'll meet you down there.'

By the time he'd ducked under the ivy that threatened to block the path and pushed the heavy back door open, she was already in the spacious basement kitchen, filling the kettle. She heard the squeak of his soles on the tiles and left the tap running as she rushed over to give him a hug.

Her soft lips brushed his cheek. Touching her had seemed so natural only a few days ago, yet now he couldn't find the proper place to put his hands. He eased out of her arms and sat down on a stool near a breakfast bar.

She turned the tap off and clicked the kettle on. 'I'm very flattered you raced over here in your lunch break to see me.'

Jake shifted his weight on the stool. 'I have some important news.'

News you're not going to like.

'Good news or bad news?'

He didn't answer. She stopped getting cups out of the cupboard and took a good look at him. 'It's bad news, isn't it it?'

'Good news, really,' he said, trying to smile. 'It just feels like bad news.'

That was the truth. He didn't want to do this, but he had no other option. He really liked her, and had hoped they'd continue to see each other for quite a while, but he'd seen the way she'd looked at the jewellery box the other night. It had taken him completely by surprise.

He'd thought he'd been safe from all of that with her. It had been short-sighted of him to go over the top with her birthday celebrations, but he'd enjoyed watching her face light up at each revelation.

So stupid of him to think he could do all that and not give her the wrong impression! She was a woman, after all. And, just like any other woman, she wanted more than he could possibly give. He was almost cross at her for making him believe otherwise.

'Jake, you're starting to worry me! Is somebody ill?'

'No. Nothing like that. It's just…I've been thinking about this for a while, and I know the time is right…'

She waved him on. 'And?'

'I'm opening a branch of my firm in New York.'

'But that's wonderful!' Pride in him radiated from her in bucketloads. He felt like something that should be scraped off on the door mat.

'There's a catch.'

'Oh?'

'I'm going to have to spend a lot of time over there in the next few months. In fact, I'm due to fly out tomorrow and I won't be back until mid-January.'

Her cheeks paled. 'Not even for Christmas?'

'No. Mum and Mel might fly out for a visit, but I won't be back.'

'Then…when will I see you?'

'This is what I wanted to talk to you about.' He looked

down at his bunched fists on the counter and deliberately
splayed his fingers. Looking her in the eye was harder than
it should have been. He'd given similar speeches before, but
he'd never felt this awkward. He took a deep breath and
squared his shoulders. He wasn't going to wimp out now.
'I'm not going to have much time for anything but the new
office for a while, so I think we should cool things off for a
bit.'

Her mouth dropped open, then she inhaled and looked
away. She hadn't seen that one coming. 'Just exactly how
cold are we talking about?'

Cruel to be kind, remember! Tell her.

'I don't think we should see each other any more. Long-
distance relationships never work.'

'They can if you want them to. And you're not going to
be gone for ever. There's the phone, and e-mail…' She trailed
off. 'Oh. Stupid me. This is a brush-off.'

'I—'

'Don't bother, Jake. I can smell that kind of crap a mile
off. I've heard it enough times to know when I'm sniffing the
genuine article.'

He didn't know what else to say. All he could do was look
at her angry, flushed face while his stomach churned.

'What's the real reason?'

'I'm going to be busy—'

She marched over to him and leaned across the counter to
look him in the eye. 'I want the truth.'

He stared into her beautiful chocolate eyes. She was right.
She didn't deserve side-stepping and half-truths. He could
have waited a few more months to open the New York branch,
and even then he needn't have stayed away for so long.

'You really want the truth?'

'I really do.'

'You're not going to like it.'

'I don't care. It's got to be better than playing second fiddle to four walls and a fax machine! I thought we had something, Jake. Something special.'

'We do—we did. But it's just not going to work out. It's better to end it now, before anyone gets hurt.'

Her eyes narrowed. She bit her lip and shook her head.

Okay, that had been stupid. She was hurt already. He knew that. That was why he was cutting her loose, to make sure he didn't do any more damage. And yet this goodbye was almost as hard on him as it was on her. This time he wouldn't be walking away without a backward glance. He was really going to miss Serena—her sense of fun, her warmth and openness, the sense that there was always another mystery waiting to be unravelled.

Then he knew why ending it with her was so hard. He'd never felt like this before, not even with Chantelle. Never considered the possibility that there was a woman out there who matched him completely. But here she was, standing in front of him, and if anything it made walking away worse. It was easy to waltz through life, believing he had immunised himself against fairytales, but it wasn't so easy to walk away knowing that if things were different—if *he* were different— he could have had it all.

The phrase 'if only' kept echoing in his head. If only he could believe in fairytales. If only he could make her truly happy. If only…

She wanted honesty? She was going to get it. Even if it left him feeling naked. He owed her that.

'You thought I had something else in that little black velvet box, didn't you?'

Her lips started to form a denial, but the words never left her mouth. She let out a puff of air. Colour crept into her cheeks and she stared at the floor.

'Is that so terrible?'

'No. It's just…' God, he wanted to haul her into his arms and tell her everything would be okay. But he couldn't. It never would be where they were concerned. 'I'm not the marrying kind, Serena. I don't have it in me.'

She looked up, shocked, as if she'd never considered the possibility that, deep down, everybody didn't hunger for a soul mate.

'How do you know unless you try?' Her voice was soft and shaky. He knew it was taking all the guts she had to ask him that.

'I just know. It wouldn't be fair to carry on.'

She covered her mouth with her hand. A tear rolled down her face.

'If I really thought I could do the lifelong commitment thing, there's no one I've come closer to wanting it with—'

'Stop!' Her voice broke, and she took a large gulp before she continued. 'I don't want to hear any more.'

She walked over to the door and held it open for him. He hesitated, then decided to do as she asked. There was nothing he could do to make it better. She kept her head turned away from him. He kissed her lightly on the cheek, hoping it would say all the sorrys he wanted to. She squeezed her eyes shut as the tears started to run in thick trails.

He stepped though the door into the bleak winter sunshine. It slammed behind him, and as he walked up the alleyway he could hear her sobbing.

Serena grabbed the alarm clock from the bedside table, threw it somewhere else, and burrowed back under the duvet.

The ringing continued.

She poked her nose out and opened one eye to look at the clock. It wasn't there. Somewhere in her sleep-fog she knew there was a good reason it wasn't sitting next to the lamp, but she had no idea what that reason might be. The clanging of the alarm against her eardrums was making any efforts at conscious thought impossible.

Hair fell in front of her face as she propped herself up and tried to get her bearings. That was the thing about sitting up half the night crying into your cocoa—when you finally got to sleep, it was next to impossible to wake up again.

She spotted the alarm clock against the skirting under the window. The battery and casing lay a few feet away. Then what on earth…?

Phone.

She grabbed the receiver of the clunky old-fashioned phone next to her bed and jammed it against her ear. 'Yes?'

'Ren? Is that you?'

'Cass? What are you doing, calling at this godawful hour?'

'It's ten-thirty.'

'It can't be.'

'Well, it is. Look at the clock.'

Easier said than done.

'Okay, okay, it's ten-thirty. Where's the fire?'

'You were supposed to be here at ten, remember?'

Oops!

'Sorry. It slipped my mind.'

'Well, it can slide right back in again, then, can't it? I thought your New Year's resolution was to find something to do while your dad is in rehab.'

Serena flumped back on the pillows and flopped the duvet over her face, phone still clamped to her ear. 'That was almost a month ago. Everyone knows that New Year's resolutions expire on January the third—the fifth at the latest.'

'Well, you said you would help with the youth music project, and I'm counting on you, resolution or not.'

'You don't really need me. After all, what can I do? I don't know anything about kids. All I know is the music industry. I'd probably just be a liability.'

'I've had enough. It's exactly *because* you work in the music industry that you're going to be useful. It's a *music* project, remember? And they're teenagers, not toddlers. You'll be fine. To be honest, I think it's about time you stopped wallowing.'

Serena stared at the rose-printed fabric in front of her nose. 'I'm not wallowing.'

'Then sit up, take the duvet off your head, and get out of bed.'

Serena stuck her tongue out at the phone. That was the trouble with best friends. They knew too much.

'I'm allowed to be a little depressed. I loved him.'

She heard Cassie sigh. 'I know you think you did, but you didn't really know him.'

'I knew enough.'

'Not enough to know he didn't want to settle down and produce your football team for you. I would have thought that was a pretty important piece of info to have.'

Serena was going to say she *had* known, because Jake had seemed so...

She punched a fist against the duvet above her head while she tried to think of the word she was looking for. It was on the tip of her tongue...

Then it hit her. She'd said it herself. It was all about how Jake had *seemed* to her, the assumptions she'd made. Nothing he'd said, or done, had ever given her the impression he'd been looking for marriage. He'd just looked the part, ticked all the right boxes.

Pity she hadn't noticed that, somewhere in the small print, the *ready for commitment* box was glaringly empty. She closed her eyes and groaned. Had she really been more in love with the idea of Jake than the real man?

'Ren?'

'Sorry, Cass. Miles away.'

'Just be here by twelve, will you?' Cassie's voice had softened, but Serena knew she wouldn't leave her alone until she'd bucked herself up. There was no arguing with Cass when she got all matron-like.

'Okay, okay. See you later.'

She pushed the duvet away and let the receiver drop back into its cradle with a satisfying thunk. She swung her legs out of bed and sat staring at the wall. The floor was cold against her bare feet.

She couldn't stay in bed all day, moping about Jake. She had to do something before the pity party spiralled out of control. As it was, she'd probably pushed the share price of Cadbury's up single-handedly.

The house was totally silent. She could hear nothing but the ebb and flow of her own breath. For months she'd been badgering her dad to go into rehab. Now he was there, the house felt the size of the Albert Hall. She hadn't realised how much time and energy it took minding her dad until now, when it was somebody else's job for a bit. And, if things worked out, he wouldn't need her as much when he came back home in six weeks' time. What was she going to do?

She thought back to the conversation she'd had with Jake in the park that day. Running away with the circus was still an option. She smiled. A maverick tear escaped from one eye and dripped onto her pyjamas, and the brick of lead that had been substituted for her heart contracted.

I miss you, Jake.

But he was right. She had a life to lead. She needed to find some other purpose than running around after her father. And while she was working out what that was, she might as well go and help Cassie with *her* mission in life.

'Grab the bag from the boot and follow me.'

Serena did as instructed, then jumped back as the car's

central locking system beeped. Only when Cassie turned a corner round a dingy block of 1960s houses did she start to jog after her.

'Cass, wait!'

Cassie stopped to let her catch up, then set off again at a blistering pace.

'Where are we? I thought this youth thingy was going to happen in the church hall.'

'Steve's decided if we really want to reach the kids on these estates, we can't expect them to walk into a stuffy old church.'

Stuffy? Hah! They could hear the electric guitar and drums three streets away when Steve was leading a service.

'St Peter's has the least stuffy services I've ever been to.'

Cass grinned with pride. 'I know that, and you know that, but the kids that live here don't. We've decided to revamp the old community centre here on this estate for the youth music project. If the mountain won't come to Mohammed…'

'I think you're mixing your faiths up.'

Cassie waved her objection away. 'It's the same principle.'

They stopped outside a low, graffiti-covered building in the shadow of a great tower block. The community centre had a row of narrow safety-glass windows that circled the building. Despite the grilles protecting them, every single one was broken.

'You can't mean to use *this* place.'

'We can. All it needs is a sweep-out, and a bit of a clean today. The glazier and carpenter are coming tomorrow, and then we're going to get busy with some paintbrushes. We have exactly a week to get this place ship-shape.'

'You keep saying "we".'

'Too right. Don't chicken out on me now, darlin'.'

Serena sighed and looked up at the neighbouring block of flats as Cassie unlocked the doors. Her heart skipped a beat.

This was Jake's estate.

He'd pointed out these very towers the afternoon they'd picnicked in the park. She glanced between the three blocks of flats that dominated the housing estate, but she had no idea which one had been his.

Cass's voice echoed from inside the community centre. 'Are you coming, or are you going to stand there all day and admire the scenery?' Serena followed her inside just in time to catch the pair of thick yellow rubber gloves that Cassie had flung in her direction. 'I'll move this old furniture out and you can sweep up.'

She pulled the gloves on and picked up a broom that was resting against the wall. She needed time to assimilate this new information, and she might as well do something mindless while she did so.

A couple of hours passed quickly as they immersed themselves in their tasks. Serena couldn't dispel the uncomfortable feeling she got from being on the Ellwood Green estate. It was as if she were trespassing. She couldn't help thinking Jake wouldn't like it if he knew she was here.

When they stopped for a break, Serena stared out of a jagged hole in one of the windows.

'That person's popular,' she said over her shoulder to Cassie.

'Who?'

'The person in that flat up there, on the second balcony. Quite a few people have gone in and out in the last hour.'

Cassie peered through a hole in the neighbouring window. 'I think I know who it belongs to.'

'You do?'

'He's definitely *not* the most likeable guy on the estate.'

'Then how come he's got so many visitors?'

Cassie slung an arm over her shoulder and shook her head. 'You really do live in the proverbial ivory tower, don't you?'

'What do you mean?'

'He's a dealer. Drugs.'

Serena gasped. 'But some of them are kids! Barely old enough to be out of primary school!'

Cassie shrugged. 'They use the local kids as look-outs and runners. In a couple of years' time, those same kids will be part of the network, earning them even more cash when they sell to their school-friends.'

She stared at Cassie in disbelief. 'I don't understand why they get mixed up with people like that in the first place.'

Cassie dragged her out through the front door and turned her to face the car park nearby. 'See that big black BMW parked over there?'

She nodded.

'It's his—the dealer's. He's well-known round here. The kids in this place grow up with next to nothing. They see this guy, with his designer clothes, thick gold jewellery and flash cars, and they want it too. You can't blame them, really. They don't want to be stuck here for the rest of their lives, on the dole or in dead-end jobs like their parents. Who wants to wipe greasy tables or pick up rubbish for a living? Mr Big up there is the only role-model for success they see at close range.'

'That's so sad.'

'Exactly,' said Cassie, slapping a cloth into her hand. 'That's why this project is so important. It might not be much, but it's a start. We can show them there's something better to do with their time, that they have other options.'

Serena's face settled into a mask of determination. 'Let's go, then! What do you want me to do next?'

Cassie grinned and handed her a huge bottle of cream cleaner. 'See that little kitchen over there…?'

Serena had an epiphany while she scrubbed.

Her childhood might not have been perfect, but it could have been a hell of a lot worse! So she'd lost her mother. At least she'd had twelve good years before her mum died. Some of the kids on this estate had probably never even met their fathers.

She scraped frantically at a bit of burnt-on grime on the electric hob. She'd spent a lot of her life feeling rather sorry for herself, when really she had so much to be thankful for. The lyrics from some of Steve's 'happy-clappy' songs suddenly made a lot more sense.

The little kitchenette gleamed. Serena stood back with her hands on her hips and surveyed her work, glad she'd forced herself out of bed that morning. Okay, glad Cassie had forced her out of bed that morning. Helping Cass had given her an unexpected dose of perspective.

She wiped her forehead with the glove-free part of her arm. 'I need some fresh air,' she called.

Cassie appeared, with a full dustpan and brush in her hand. The dust in her hair had turned it a rather dirty shade of pink. 'I need something cold and fizzy. Do you want to nip out to the newsagents and get us something to drink?'

Serena peeled her gloves off and left them on the counter. 'Where is it?'

'Follow the path to the left, past the nearest block of flats. When you come to the end, go left again and you should see a row of shops.'

Serena nodded, checked her jeans pocket for change, then walked out into the bright January afternoon.

She had been walking for less than a minute when she became aware of someone behind her. Not too close, but close enough, keeping pace almost. She slowed down a little to give whoever it was a chance to overtake. The footsteps matched her own.

Her heart began to thump even before she picked up speed again.

This was ridiculous! It was probably some old lady on her

way to the bingo. But if that were the case why was she scared to turn round and take a look?

She wanted to break into a jog. Instead, she tightened her stomach muscles and glanced quickly over her shoulder, hoping to be rewarded by a nod from an old dear in a tweed coat.

It was a man.

More than that was hard to say. His woollen hat was pulled down over his ears and a scarf was knotted round his neck, covering his chin and mouth. He'd burrowed even further into the turned-up collar of his scruffy grey overcoat when she'd sneaked a look at him.

He wasn't doing anything threatening, wasn't getting any closer, but it just didn't feel right. Her palms itched and cold air sliced her throat as she drew it into her lungs.

They were almost in the shadow of the tower. The path ran right next to the block of flats, under the overhanging balconies of the upper floors. It looked as if it was designed to be a shelter for the entrance, but it felt as if she would be hemmed in after the open space of the walkway. The only alternative was to turn and face him, and she certainly didn't want to do that!

Suddenly she was running towards twenty storeys of concrete and dirty glass. She shoved one of the heavy double doors open and jabbed a finger on the lift button, taking care to breathe through her mouth. The foyer reeked like a public toilet.

She glanced outside, through the glass-panelled doors. He was getting closer, but it was impossible to tell if he was just going to walk past or follow her inside.

The lift machinery was ominously silent. No distant *dings* of the lift on upper floors. No lights on the display. She pressed the button one last time, then darted up the staircase without waiting for a result. The sound of her footsteps bounced off the walls in the confined space. She counted off thirty steps then stopped, a foot poised on the next step so she was ready to set off again.

Nothing. No sound behind her. It would have been hard to climb those stairs without making a noise. She slouched against the wall and caught her breath.

What to do now? She didn't want to go back downstairs just yet and risk running into the grey overcoat. She glanced up the stairs.

Fourteenth floor, Jake had said.

Her feet set up a rhythm on the stairs again, slower this time.

Each landing looked like the last. The floor numbers on the walls were often obscured by neon spray paint. Nothing artistic, though. Just name tags and obscene phrases. Finally, she stood beside the plaque reading '14' and gulped oxygen into her lungs, her calf muscles screaming.

Her destination was a bit of an anticlimax. Somehow she'd thought she would have a sense of arrival, that something in the narrow corridor would shout, *Jake was here!* But all she saw was a row of identical blue doors. At the end of the corridor was a large window. She walked up to it and looked out on Jake's world.

The greyness seemed to spread in every direction from the base of the block of flats for miles and miles. The oasis of Greenwich Park was nowhere to be seen. She must be looking in the wrong direction.

In her imagination, she tried to picture Jake as he would have been fifteen years ago—baggy jeans with rips and a baseball cap. Would his dark hair have been longer and shaggier, or would it have been a crew cut? The image wouldn't come. She could only see him in crisp shirts and designer suits, his hair neat, never a tuft sticking up. She didn't know the Jake of Ellwood Green at all.

But she understood *her* Jake better—the need to succeed

at his career, his love of fine things and first-class service. It was a world away from the scene she looked down upon now. He'd talked about how he'd wanted to escape, and he'd done it. She admired him for that. It was a testament to his drive and determination that *his* BMW was parked in the underground garage of his office, and not in the car park downstairs as he waited for the next knock on the front door.

She walked back to the stairwell and started her descent. Once at ground level, she stayed well back from the doors and searched for any sign of a grey coat. When she was sure it was safe, she eased the door open and peeked out, grateful for the relief from the acrid stench of the foyer.

No sign. She let out a large breath and waited, half-in, half-out the door, for another minute before setting off again.

It wasn't long before she spotted the small parade of shops. The newsagents sat between a boarded-up unit and a launderette.

She picked a couple of bottles out of the cold cabinet inside and took them to the counter. A pair of chatting teenage girls hushed and watched her hand over the coins to the shop-keeper. She stuffed her change into her back pocket and scurried out of the shop.

Jake's roots were here. It was his world. And she clearly didn't belong.

Jake rested his elbows on the bar of the trolley and scanned the luggage carousel for his cases. A willowy blonde woman on the other side of the conveyor belt made eye contact. Normally he would have stood up and smiled, but instead he picked a case to watch and pretended he hadn't seen her.

London was a big city, but a homing beacon was calling out to him. His mind was tuned to wherever *she* was. It had been the same in New York. A little *blip-blip-blip* constantly on his radar. And now he was home, it was stronger than ever.

CHAPTER SIX

ICY rain battered the windows of the community hall. Serena looked over to Cassie and sighed. It was eight o'clock already and no one had turned up, just like last week.

She glanced across at Mel, Cassie's project worker, who had propped her elbows on the coffee bar and rested her chin in her hands. Her heartstrings twanged unexpectedly. Mel looked so much like her brother—the same dark hair, blue eyes and intense expression—but, unlike Jake, Mel wore her heart on her sleeve. She didn't lock a little part of herself away from the world and smooth over the cracks with a smile.

It didn't matter. Where Jake wore his heart and what he did with it was none of her business. He was four thousand miles away. She closed her eyes and willed herself to think of something else.

Steve suddenly stood up from the stool he'd been perched on. 'We're going to have to call in reinforcements, gang! It's half term in two weeks, and we want the daily workshops full.'

'How are we going to do that?' Serena looked at the circle of empty chairs. 'It's going to take a miracle.'

A slow smile spread across Steve's face. 'Miracles are my speciality—or, in this case, yours.'

'Mine?'

'I don't know why I didn't think of it before! Your dad must have tons of contacts in the music business. Can you think of someone—*anyone*—who would help us out? We need a name. Someone to attract the kids.'

Serena looked at the ceiling and scrunched up her face. A couple of seconds passed and she smiled back at Steve.

'Actually, I *can* think of someone. And he owes me—big time. You'll get your name, Steve, and in time for the launch too. I guarantee it.'

Cassie bounded over and rested her chin on Serena's shoulder. 'Who is it, then?'

Serena just tapped her nose with her finger and said nothing.

Just when he'd thought he was wise to her tricks, she'd gone and done it again!

Jake stared at the phone on his desk and shook his head. One minute he'd been sorting his e-mails and listening to Mel yatter on about a great pair of boots she'd just bought, and the next he'd agreed to take a week of mornings off work for some project of hers.

He was going to have to insist on doing all communication with his sister face-to-face. She was getting far too clever.

'I can't believe it! I'm such a big fan of yours.'

Cassie was gushing. Honest-to-goodness, eighteen-carat gushing. It wouldn't be long before she shook the mystery guest's hand off. The guy didn't know what had hit him. Serena almost felt sorry for him.

She smiled to herself. And why not? She was feeling very pleased she'd bagged an up-and-coming R&B star for the Saturday night launch of Music Week. He would generate a lot of publicity. Not only that, but he was leading a few work-shops too. The estate grapevine had gone into overdrive and the community centre was packed. She studied the assorted crowd. Council dignitaries stood shoulder-to-shoulder with baggy-trousered teenagers.

Cassie finally let go of the poor man's hand. 'How ever did you manage this?' she asked Serena, eyes firmly fixed on the man flexing and stretching his fingers.

If only she knew! Who would have guessed those tortur-ous hours babysitting little Kevin would have paid off in the end?

Big Kevin's voice was gruff in her ear. 'Yes, how *did* you wangle this one?'

'Shut up, Kevin,' she said through a clenched smile. 'Or I'll tell everyone how you used to do ballroom dancing in sparkly red jumpsuits.'

He glowered at her. 'That's blackmail.'

'Blackmail is such an ugly word. I prefer to think of it as reparation for the many pranks you played on me over the years.' Those dark times when her dad and Kevin's parents had partied until dawn and left her in charge of a twelve-year-old with a death wish. She punched his arm in mock cheer-fulness. 'Remember when you *borrowed* my car and left it with an empty tank in Soho? Ah, those were the days.'

He grunted.

She hummed a bar or two of a Viennese waltz.

'Smile, *Kevin*, everybody's watching.'

'It's Daddy K to you.'

'Whatever.'

She tucked her arm into his and they turned to face the gathering crowd, their smiles little more than bared teeth.

A shiver crawled up Serena's spine. Someone was watching her—which was an absurd thing to think. At least two hundred people had their eyes trained on her and the boy wonder, but it still felt as if, somewhere in the crowd, a pair of eyes was pinning her down.

Her ivy earrings swung as she whipped her head around and met his stare.

Jake.

Her heart performed a perfect swan dive and burrowed into the toes of her boots. Never in a million years had she expected to see him here. The ghost of yesteryear, maybe, echoes of Jake that lurked in the stairwells and playground, but never the new, updated and improved version. She'd thought she'd be safe here.

Why? Why was he here? It made no sense. He'd run away so fast from this place there were still skid marks on the pavement.

Then she caught sight of Mel, looking from her to Jake and back again, and she knew why. What chance did they have against the combined forces of Cassie and Mel? Were they trying to set them up again, as if nothing had happened? Unbelievable! She was going to wipe that soppy look off Mel's face the first opportunity she got.

She looked back towards the door. It was still open. A couple of steps and she'd be out of there, running as fast as her high-heeled boots could take her.

Kevin—she refused to call him by his ridiculous stage name—tugged her forward as he approached a man in a wrinkled suit. But her boots stayed glued to the floor. She recognised the man as a local councillor who'd suddenly decided to champion the project now he had the chance of seeing his face in the paper.

Kevin took another step forward and her arm slid free of his, leaving her standing alone in the middle of the hall. The words *sitting* and *duck* came to mind.

Don't look at him. Don't look at him!

Oh, you spineless creature!

Jake hadn't moved a muscle. He was leaning against the wall, his brows crinkled together, giving Daddy K the evil eye.

He's jealous?

That was rich, considering who had dumped who! She straightened and stared at him until he made eye contact. Once that small victory was accomplished, she nudged forward and slid her arm into Kevin's again.

One of the helpers brushed past her.

'Michelle, could you shut that door for me, please? It's letting all the cold air in.'

The girl nodded and scurried away.

No more Miss Puffy-Eyed Wimp! She dug her heels into the ancient lino and did her best to ignore the heat of Jake's eyes boring into the back of her head.

An hour later the music was still pumping. Kevin was performing a couple of songs, and Serena felt like a three-year-old without her security blanket. She jostled her way through the crowd to the non-alcoholic bar and grabbed a bottle of mineral water. Then, just as she was elbowing her way out of the crush, she came face to face with the man she'd been doing her best to avoid.

Why did he have to look so gorgeous? Couldn't he have grown an extra head or broken out in boils in the last couple of months?

'Hello, Serena.' That much was easy to lip-read.

Hello, worm.

'Hello, Jake,' she shouted back.

He said something else, but she couldn't make half of it out through the throbbing music.

'Pardon?'

He leant in close to speak into her ear. After eight weeks and five days of no contact, he was pushing her into sensory overload. Not only was his breath warming her cheek, but he smelled so good! Like crisp clean shirts with a hint of after-shave.

'How have you been?'

It was just as well his questions were as inane as the answers that whirred through her head. He was far too close to make sparkling repartee a possibility. She would just be happy if her mouth moved and sound came out.

'Fine. You?'

'Fine.'

Both their pants should be on fire, figuratively speaking. She'd never seen him look so tense. Where was the effort-less charm? Had he checked it in at Customs when he returned?

'We can't talk here.' His voice was just that little bit too loud in her ear and she pulled away.

'Who says we've got anything left to say to each other?'

She gave him what she hoped was a scorching look then wove her way over to the other side of the room. She undid the lid on her bottle of water and took a gulp.

'I don't want to leave things like this between us.' They were now far enough from the speakers for her to decipher his yelling.

She should have guessed he wouldn't give up that easily. On some level she'd wanted him to follow her, wanted a chance to vent her anger. The imaginary conversations she'd been having with him since Christmas could now become a reality. Perhaps then the words would stop circuiting her head as if it were a racetrack.

She screwed the lid back on her water bottle so tight the ridges burned her fingers. 'Don't pretend you care, Jake. You're the one who ended it, remember? Just be glad I'm moving on instead of stalking you.'

'Moving on?' He flashed a quick look at Kevin and the

heaving mass of girls trying to storm the makeshift stage. 'You know it's not that I didn't like you—'

Serena lifted her chin and stretched her lips into a smile. 'Save it for someone who cares, Charlie.'

His jaw clenched so tight she thought his teeth would shatter. She'd hit a nerve. Good!

'You're a fake. Do you know that, Jake?'

She would swear she could actually hear his blood bubbling in response to that. Or perhaps it was the steady bass beat of Kevin's song.

'*Me?* A fake?'

'Yes, you. You look like a decent, caring man, but—' her voice was getting shrill '—but underneath you're a commitment-phobic coward like the rest of your species!' She finished her tirade and froze.

Everyone was staring at them. At her. And the music had stopped. While her lips twitched and she wondered how to dissolve into nothing, Jake grabbed her arm and yanked her out through the door.

He didn't need to shout outside. The barely contained whisper he used next was far more lethal. Her confidence evaporated.

'I didn't ever pretend to be anything I'm not. What are us guys supposed to do? Wear little flashing neon signs saying "Husband Material"? You jumped to your happy-ever-after conclusions all on your own. You saw what you wanted to see.'

Words tripped over her tongue and fell flat before they passed her teeth. What could she say? Jake smiled, but not one of his heart-melting ones. This one was cold and brittle, but his voice still came out even and normal. She hated the fact he could do that when all she could manage were squeaks and screeches.

'Anyway, you seem to have *moved on* to new pastures—

GET FREE BOOKS and FREE GIFTS
WHEN YOU PLAY THE...

SLOT MACHINE GAME!

Just scratch off the silver box with a coin. Then check below to see the gifts you get!

YES! I have scratched off the silver box. Please send me the 2 free Silhouette Romance® books and 2 free gifts for which I qualify. I understand I am under no obligation to purchase any books, as explained on the back of this card.

310 SDL EF35   **210 SDL EF4W**

FIRST NAME	LAST NAME

ADDRESS

APT.#	CITY

STATE/ PROV.	ZIP/POSTAL CODE

7	7	7	**Worth TWO FREE BOOKS plus 2 BONUS Mystery Gifts!**
🍒	🍒	🍒	**Worth TWO FREE BOOKS!**
♣	♣	♣	**Worth ONE FREE BOOK!**
🔔	🔔	🍒	**TRY AGAIN!**

www.eHarlequin.com

(S-R-12/06)

Offer limited to one per household and not valid to current Silhouette Romance® subscribers.

Your Privacy - Silhouette Books is committed to protecting your privacy. Our Privacy Policy is available online at www.eHarlequin.com or upon request from the Silhouette Reader Service. From time to time we make our lists of customers available to reputable firms who may have a product or service of interest to you. If you would prefer for us not to share your name and address, please check here ☐.

© 2000 HARLEQUIN ENTERPRISES LTD. ® and TM are trademarks owned and used by the trademark owner and/or its licensee.

DETACH AND MAIL CARD TODAY!

The Silhouette Reader Service™ — Here's how it works:

Accepting your 2 free books and 2 free mystery gifts places you under no obligation to buy anything. You may keep the books and gifts and return the shipping statement marked "cancel." If you do not cancel, about a month later we'll send you 4 additional books and bill you just $3.57 each in the U.S., or $4.05 each in Canada, plus 25¢ shipping & handling per book and applicable taxes if any.* That's the complete price and — compared to cover prices of $4.25 each in the U.S. and $4.99 each in Canada — it's quite a bargain! You may cancel at any time, but if you choose to continue, every month we'll send you 4 more books, which you may either purchase at the discount price or return to us and cancel your subscription.

*Terms and prices subject to change without notice. Sales tax applicable in N.Y. Canadian residents will be charged applicable provincial taxes and GST. All orders subject to approval. Credit or debit balances in a customer's account(s) may be offset by any other outstanding balance owed by or to the customer. Please allow 4 to 6 weeks for delivery.

If offer card is missing write to: Silhouette Reader Service, 3010 Walden Ave., P.O. Box 1867, Buffalo NY 14240-1867

BUSINESS REPLY MAIL
FIRST-CLASS MAIL   PERMIT NO. 717-003   BUFFALO, NY

POSTAGE WILL BE PAID BY ADDRESSEE

SILHOUETTE READER SERVICE
3010 WALDEN AVE
PO BOX 1867
BUFFALO NY 14240-9952

NO POSTAGE
NECESSARY
IF MAILED
IN THE
UNITED STATES

or should I say happy hunting grounds? I hope the poor sucker knows what he's letting himself in for.'

'You arrogant—' She stopped herself before she said something really unladylike. 'What's so wrong with wanting a husband and a family? It's hardly abnormal! Isn't that what everyone's searching for—a little love and happiness?'

Jake stopped smiling and looked sheepish.

All the rage was suddenly sucked out of her. Why couldn't it have been him? Life was so unfair! She took a deep breath and tried to disguise her quivering lip by bowing her head.

He gently tipped her face up again by lifting her chin with his finger. 'Let's not fight. It's pointless. I've told you before that you're a unique woman, Serena. You're right, you deserve the love and happiness you're looking for.'

Oh, this was worse! His anger she could handle, but his pity…?

'Just not with you.'

'No.'

'Why not?' If she was going to embarrass herself past the point of no return, she might as well get the whole lot off her chest.

'I wouldn't make you happy. I'd break your heart.'

Too late. It's a done deal.

'How do you know unless you try?'

'I did try once. It was a complete disaster. I'm not about to mess up anyone else's life like that.'

Her stomach clenched at the thought of Jake with someone else, of him loving someone else. It wasn't that he *couldn't* commit, just that he wouldn't with her.

'There's not much I can say to that, is there?'

Jake ran his fingers through his hair. 'Look, I'm taking time off work this week, to help with some of the workshops, and if we're going to be around each other we're going to have to find a way to co-exist harmoniously.'

She sighed and nodded. He was right again, and it made her want to box his ears for being all reasonable and logical when her heart was fracturing into cold, solid lumps.

'Okay. Truce.' She offered him a hand and he took it, but instead of shaking it he just stood there looking at it, his fingers blistering her skin. Then his thumb brushed against the back of her hand, giving her a jolt of raw awareness.

They both continued to look at their joined hands.

He felt it too. He must do. For all his sane words, he was no more immune to the chemistry between them than she was. She looked up at him and saw the truth of it in his eyes as he leaned in to kiss her.

She knew she should push him away, but instead of resisting him with the hand that had flown to his chest, she slid it up behind his neck and pulled him closer.

Once they started kissing, they couldn't seem to stop. She'd kissed him many times in the few weeks they'd gone out, but this one had an edge to it. There was a hunger and a quiet desperation from him that had never been evident before. He kissed her like a drowning man gasping for air, as if he needed it to survive. Her foolish heart leapt at the knowledge.

It was Jake who dragged himself away first. She rested her head against his shoulder, eyes still closed, and tasted him on her lips with her tongue. The courage to open her lids and look him in the face was nowhere to be found.

'I'm sorry, Serena. I shouldn't have done that. It was wrong to let…'

His voice was heavy with regret. If only the concrete slabs beneath her feet would open up and swallow her.

'What I was trying to say…before…was that we should try to remain civil—be friends, even.'

Oh, he really had no clue, did he?

Still, she nodded, opened her eyes and stared resolutely

at his chest. Her hand was pressed against it again. She snatched it away.

'Of course. Friends.'

Then he turned and walked back inside, leaving her to prop herself up against the rough-plastered wall and wonder why she hadn't noticed sooner how cold it was outside.

Serena looked at her watch for the fifteenth time. Eighteen minutes past eight, Monday morning, and she was at the community centre, setting up for the day ahead. Mel had nipped out to the local shop to buy some more coffee, so she unstacked the chairs in blissful silence.

Come to think of it, Mel had been gone an awfully long time.

She stuck her head out through the front door and did a quick scan of the surrounding area. Mel's pink coat was visible some distance away. Her head was bobbing up and down furiously as she talked to a man in grey.

A cold wave crashed in Serena's tummy.

A grey coat. Just like the man who had followed her the other day. What if Mel was in trouble? She was just about to shove the door wider and race over there when Mel gave the man a hug and headed back in her direction.

Serena peered at the stranger. He had his back to her, and it was impossible to tell if it was the same person. This man wasn't wearing a hat and scarf. The only similarities were the colour of his coat and his height.

She shrugged and shook her head. Mel obviously wasn't bothered by him. She was probably just imagining things. Her nerves were wire-tight. It was hardly surprising if she was dreaming up trouble where there was none.

She let the door flap closed and returned to setting up the chairs and instruments for the 'Guitar for Dummies' workshop. Mel had shanghaied Jake into leading that one.

She checked her watch again. Another thirty-eight minutes and he'd be here. She stood, chair held mid-air, and wished the sick feeling in her stomach away.

The thup-thup of the swing door announced Mel's return.

'I can't believe Mr Singh still runs the corner shop! I was always a little scared of him as a child, but he practically vaulted over the counter to shake my hand just now.'

'You were a long time.'

Mel paused. 'Yes…well, like I said, I was catching up with Mr Singh.'

'Who was the other man you were talking to?'

'What man?' Mel fiddled with her top button.

'The one in the grey coat.'

'Oh, him. That was no one. He was just asking for directions.'

Serena raised an eyebrow as Mel shrugged off her coat and busied herself putting the jar of coffee away.

Jake looked at the circle of faces in front of him and inwardly winced. A dozen or so teenage boys and girls were staring at him, waiting for him to impress them. He was having fantasies of making a break for it and leaving a Jake-shaped hole in the nearest wall. He'd been less terrified when Lord and Lady Balfour had summoned him to their castle to discuss streamlining their estate's finances.

Five hours of workshops this week—and there were four hours and fifty-six minutes left to go. The second hand of the badly hung clock couldn't clunk through the seconds fast enough. Then he could get out of this hellhole and back to his real life.

Knowing *she* was watching him didn't help. She was trying to pretend she wasn't watching, but she was. She was just as attuned to him as he was to her. He risked a look across at Serena. Her head was buried in a stack of registration forms. Then her pen stopped moving and she went still. A couple of seconds later she peered at him through her fringe.

See? Attuned!

The motley group in front of him began to get restless, and he turned his attention back to them. How did teenage girls manage that withering *you're-such-a-loser* look? It must be something to do with their overly tight ponytails.

When in doubt, he always fell back on his tried and trusted arsenal. He smiled, and the charm started to flow. It was like flicking a switch.

A loud *tut* from the desk near the door almost made him falter, but he launched seamlessly into his memorised lesson plan, starting with the basics: which end of the guitar was up.

Serena, meanwhile, sorted the registration forms into alphabetical order. Then into age order. Then by workshop choices. Anything to keep her eyes away from the far end of the hall.

The strangling of guitar strings didn't even register. All she could hear was Jake's cool voice, carefully explaining basic chords. After their initial display of expected apathy, the workshop participants had settled down, and now hung on his every word. All but one.

A boy of about fifteen slouched in his plastic chair and hardly bothered to pretend he was placing his fingers in the correct position for E minor. Max something. She flipped through the registration forms again and found his.

Max Black. Age: fourteen. Address: Ellwood Green Council Estate.

Why was he here if he wasn't interested? Oh, right. Max had been recommended by his social worker in an attempt to keep him out of trouble.

She glanced across at the boy. It was stupid to think this way, but it felt good to know that there was at least one human being immune to the charms of Charles Jacobs, Jr.

She was tempted to go and high five Max for that very fine accomplishment, because she was doing a miserable job of being immune to him herself.

With ten minutes of the workshop left, there was an outburst. Max had got fed up with acting bored, and tried to join in with the simple tune the rest of the group were strumming. Since he hadn't paid attention, his fingers tripped over the chord changes and he couldn't keep up.

Serena watched Max grind his teeth, then his face flushed deep pink—the only warning an explosion was imminent. He hurled his guitar on the floor, kicked his chair out of the way and stormed out.

The rest of the group froze, eyes wide. The gentle reverberation of the chord they'd just played hung in the air. They all looked at Jake and waited for him to go ballistic.

Of course he did nothing of the sort. He calmly righted the upturned chair, sat the dented guitar up against it, and carried on as if nothing had happened.

From her vantage point near the door, she could still see Max. He was hovering in the shadow of one of the tower blocks. He was too far away to make out his expression, but even at that distance his anger radiated in waves towards them.

She forgot to shuffle her papers and looked back at Jake. Damn him for being so totally in control of himself! She would love to see him lose it—really lose it—just once. And damn herself for wanting him more each passing day, despite his iron-clad bachelor status.

Before she'd finished lecturing herself on the pointlessness of it all, Jake had wound up the workshop and the kids had trailed back outside. He'll probably want a coffee, she thought to herself, and was just about to ask him, heart pulsating in the back of her throat, when he sprinted out through the front door, leaving her gaping.

No more than five minutes later the door crashed open and he reappeared, frog-marching Max in front of him.

'Well, Max, the damage done to the guitar is fixable, but you are going to have to work off the cost of the repairs by helping out here for the rest of the week.'

Max grunted, and glared at Jake.

Jake glared back, unmoved.

'Forget it! I'm not sticking around this dump any longer than I have to. You can take your guitar and shove it—'

'Fine. But I'm guessing that your social worker doesn't want to hear about this. I heard that you were on your last warning. But if you want me to call the police and report the incident of criminal damage that just happened here, I will be most obliged to do so.'

Max said a word no fourteen-year-old should even know, and his feet shuffled to a halt. He looked as if he'd been sentenced to fifteen years hard labour, not a few days of floor-sweeping and coffee-making. He turned to face Jake and shoved his hands in his pockets. Jake pointed at the far corner of the room.

'We need twenty chairs, in four rows of five, for the next class, and I think it's about time you made the team a cup of tea. Put the kettle on, and you can do the chairs while it boils.'

Max stomped off in the direction of the kitchen.

'You know he's going to spit in your coffee, don't you?' Serena said in a hushed voice.

Jake laughed. 'I'll give him the one he offers me.'

'You're too smooth for your own good. Do you know that?'

They smiled at each other. Serena forced herself to remember he was the enemy—the man who'd stolen her heart, decided he didn't want it, yet still refused to give it back. She was giving him permission to shred it into tiny pieces by weakening.

And still she couldn't stop smiling at him.

The number forty-seven bus trundled over London Bridge and Jake's shoulders unknotted. For years the Thames had been a physical and psychological barrier to his past. The bus was getting more and more crowded, but he didn't mind a bit. He could take anything now he was back on *his* side of the river.

He jumped out of his seat to offer it to a silver-haired lady with a string shopping bag. Taking the bus had been a stroke of genius. Who knew how long his BMW would have remained unmolested in the car park on the estate?

Oddly enough, he'd almost forgotten he'd left it at the office when he'd seen an almost identical model parked a short distance from the community centre. At first he'd thought that Max was wreaking revenge by breaking into his car. The boy's spiky black head had been bowed close to the driver's window. Only when he'd stepped away slightly had Jake seen that Max was talking to the driver through the open window, and he remembered he'd left his own car tucked up safe and snug in the underground car park.

But he'd still felt uneasy—this time on Max's behalf. He knew how much that car cost, almost down to the penny, and it wasn't anything law-abiding residents of Ellwood Green could dream of owning. Max was skating on thin ice by associating himself with that kind of man.

Then the BMW had pulled away. He'd listened to the tyres screeching round the corner as he and Max had eyed each other on opposite sides of the road. Max's first instinct had been to cower slightly, but then he'd straightened and swaggered towards him. The kid had guts. As Max had closed the distance between them he'd puffed himself up even more, looking as if he was expecting a fight.

But Jake had known that letting rip at him right then would only have done more damage. Max was much more scared than he'd let on. It was frightening how well he could read the boy. Not so long ago he'd been wired the same way. Max was angry at the world and didn't know how to curb his frustration, but, properly channelled, that drive and energy could be his path to a better future.

Jake's thoughts drifted to the look of admiration on Serena's face when he'd returned to the centre with Max. Her approval shouldn't mean anything to him. He didn't want it. He didn't need it. And anyway, he'd promised himself he wasn't going to think about her.

He squeezed the red button with his thumb and heard the ding as the 'Bus Stopping' sign lit up. He nudged his way to the exit and angled himself through the double doors as they hissed open.

His building was in sight. All he needed now was to change out of these casual clothes into his suit, and his armour would be back in place.

A vagrant was huddled in the corner of the entrance, the collar on his coat turned up and his hat pulled down against the biting wind. Security would probably move the man on shortly. Jake rummaged in his pocket for a few coins and dropped them at the man's feet.

The heavy plate-glass door was already half-open when the blood in his veins ran like ice.

'Three quid? You can do better than that for your old man. Can't you, son?'

CHAPTER SEVEN

THE door slammed closed and Jake turned to stare open-mouthed as the man pulled himself to his feet.

It had been more than ten years since he'd last seen his father, and the revulsion hit him like a shockwave, hurtling him back in time.

'I have nothing to say to you.' He'd rather pull out his own fingernails than call that man Dad. He started to shove the door open again.

'I've got a couple of words to say to you, though: *Serendipity Dove.*'

Jake stilled, raw anger pounding in his head. He turned. 'What about her?'

The slimy smile his father gave made him remember why he'd always wanted to punch him. Last time the old toad had turned up he actually had. He wasn't proud of himself, but it had been a drop in the ocean compared to his teenage years when he'd been on the receiving end. He stuffed his fists in his jacket pockets.

'A little bird told me you were an item.'

'Your little bird is out of date. It's ancient history.'

'Shame. There could have been a bit of mileage in that.'

Jake invaded his 'old man's' personal space so quickly his father took a step backwards. Soon he was backed up against the polished granite wall of the entrance, and the slimy smile started to waver.

'Now, hang on, Charlie—'

'Don't call me that! It's Jake or Charles, but *never* Charlie!' Jake got his face close enough to smell the stale tobacco on his father's breath. 'Let's get this straight. If you go anywhere near her, so help me, I'll see to it you're in no fit state to ever bother anyone again!' His fists were getting restless in the confines of his pocket, so he dug them in deeper.

'Okay, okay, it was only a thought!' His father wriggled free and put some space between them. He raised his hands in an attitude of surrender.

Jake shook his head. He knew all the guy's tricks, even after a decade. Right now he was trying to defuse the situation by oozing charm, so he could attack it from another angle. In Jake's opinion, the man oozed something entirely different.

'Come on, Charlie. We're two of a kind, you and me. I always had an eye for a pretty girl myself, you know.'

'And if I remember rightly, being married to Mum didn't slow you down at all, either.'

'Your mother and I had an arrangement.'

Jake barked out a hollow laugh. 'What? You mean the one where she stayed home and cried while you went out and gambled all our money away?'

'A man's got a right to a beer and a flutter on the gee-gees every now and then.'

Did he actually believe the rubbish he was spouting?

'It was Mum's money! Money she earned scrubbing other people's floors because you were too useless to hold down a job. Mel and I almost got taken into care after you split with all our savings. Mum only just managed to make ends meet and keep us together!'

His father looked up at the gold lettering painted on the doors to the plush foyer. '"Jacobs Associates",' he read. 'Seems like you turned out all right to me.'

'No thanks to you. Now, clear off!'

'I'd be happy to. Only funds are a little short…'

'What's the matter? Have you managed to fleece every middle-aged divorcée on the Costa Blanca?'

His father shrugged.

'I'm not giving you a penny!'

'Go on, son. Ten grand and I'll be out of your hair for good, I promise. You'll never have to see me again.'

'Your promises are worth nothing! Don't you think I know that? I meant what I said. I'm not giving you anything. Now, get lost!'

The saccharine mask dropped from his father's face, and suddenly Jake could see the real man he'd always known lurked beneath: mean, selfish and spineless.

'Go away and prey on someone else.'

'All right, I will. But don't blame me when it all comes back to bite you on the backside.'

Jake folded his arms, his back against the door as if guarding it, and watched in satisfaction as his father walked away.

'I'm nothing like you!' he shouted after him. His father didn't turn round, and Jake waited until the tatty grey overcoat had disappeared into the crowds, just to make sure he was really gone.

'Nothing like you,' he muttered as he finally pushed the door open, more angry at himself than he was at his father at that moment. Angry because he knew he was lying.

The snooker ball skittered around the rickety table, then dropped into a pocket.

'Yesss!' yelled Max, punching a fist in the air. Serena

smiled as she sat perched on her usual stool at the coffee bar. What a difference from the surly boy who had sloped into the community centre at the beginning of the week!

His next shot was not so lucky. The ball bounced off two cushions, then came to a halt two inches from the intended hole.

Jake tutted, then lined up his shot. 'You shouldn't count your chickens, boy. Now, stand back and let me show you how it's done.'

Talk about excess testosterone! Why did the males of the species have to turn every little challenge into a fight to the death?

Max grunted, but stared at his opponent with an obvious case of hero-worship. Jake had spent a lot of time with him this week. Serena had the feeling that nobody ever took time to be with Max. The positive attention was having a transforming effect on him. He was still a bit mouthy at times, but he'd arrived early the last two mornings to help set up for the day. And now he was hanging around after Jake's workshop had finished just so he could grab a few more minutes in the presence of his idol.

The really tragic thing was that Serena only knew Max had turned up early because she had done exactly the same thing. For exactly the same reason. Pathetic.

'The heart wants what the heart wants,' her mother had always said, and her heart wanted Jake, however much her head declared it folly.

Jake manoeuvred round the snooker table to take his next shot and gave her an unparalleled view of his denim-clad rear-end. She dropped her head to the counter and covered it with her arms. Why was she torturing herself like this?

Her *perfect husband* tick-list had been abandoned. Jake had both fulfilled and exceeded it. She'd been looking for safe and reliable when she'd met him, but she'd found so much more. He was passionate and imaginative and intuitive. All the things she'd thought were reserved for the 'creative types' she'd discounted from her search.

She'd always assumed that 'settling down' by definition included a certain amount of…well, *settling*. It was a trade-off. Passion and excitement versus companionship and security. Then, just when she'd been ready to make the sacrifice, she'd hit the jackpot.

Oh, but life was never that easy. It gave with one hand and took away with the other. Mr Right was, in fact, Mr Wrong. As much as she wanted him, he didn't want her back.

She banged her head on the coffee bar a few times to scatter her thoughts.

'Serena? You all right?' It was Jake's voice.

Her own came out muffled from underneath her folded arms. 'Yes, fine. Just…resting.' *Lame, lame, lame.*

The clacking of snooker balls continued. A triumphant shout confirmed that Jake had snatched victory from under Max's nose for the umpteenth time. She lifted an elbow and peeked out. Max was collecting snooker balls and throwing them into a cardboard box with more force than necessary.

'Loser makes the coffees—that's the deal. Off you go, up-start!'

Max turned to put the box away and she saw a smile he'd meant to hide from everyone else. 'Get 'em yourself, Grandpa!'

Hair fell across her face as she lifted her head, and she brushed it away with her hand. Max was stomping towards her with a couple of dirty mugs hooked on his fingers. She took them from him.

'I'll do the drinks, Max. You've worked really hard all week. Take a break.'

Instead of looking pleased, Max's face clouded over. 'It's the last day today.'

'Not looking forward to school on Monday?'

Max mimed slitting his own throat.

'Eeewww!'

He grinned, pleased with the reaction, then turned to look at Jake. 'Do you think he'll come on Friday nights?'

'I don't know. Jake says he doesn't *do* long term.'

They both lapsed into silence as they waited for the kettle to boil. Thankfully, her mobile phone rang.

'Hello?'

'I feel like hell.' It was Cassie. 'Steve got me to take a theology course last year, so I know what I'm talking about. I won't be coming in this morning. You've got enough adults to comply with all the regs, haven't you?

'Yes, of course,' she lied. Steve and Mel had dashed off to some emergency, but she wasn't going to tell Cassie that. 'You take care of yourself, and I'll drop by later.'

Serena ended the call and stared at her phone. They needed to have two adults present at all times. It was fine to tell Cassie it was all sorted, but in reality there was only one candidate for the post, and he was supposed to be heading back to work in ten minutes.

'Jake? I wouldn't ask if it wasn't an emergency, but could you hang on until Steve and Mel get back?'

'How long?'

She bit the corner of her lip. 'One-ish. Can you spare the time?'

He walked closer, too close, and looked her in the eyes. 'Sure. I'll make a call or two to smooth things over. But I have one condition.'

'I'm not playing snooker with you again. It's embarrassing.'

'Not snooker. Dinner.'

Her heels echoed on the floor as she took a step back. 'I don't think that's a good idea.'

'Why? Has nutrition suddenly gone out of fashion?' He smiled a great, cheeky smile. She could feel herself weakening. Still, she set her face into a frown and answered him. 'You know why.'

'Lunch, then? It'll be time to eat when Steve and Mel get here.'

She shook her head, not trusting her mouth to comply.

'Go on, we'll get plastic-boxed sandwiches and eat them on a bench. They'll taste nasty. You won't enjoy yourself at all.'

Her lips found a different way to betray her and curled themselves into an answering smile. 'Rubbery cheese and hard white bread?'

'Deal.'

They were just going to eat sandwiches together. Friends did that sort of thing. The singing workshop was starting up. Rick, the choir leader from Steve's church, was teaching a group of twenty or so to sing like a gospel choir. They were making good progress. The main group had the harmonies licked, but the soloist was having trouble.

'Darren, you have to fit your part over the top of the choir, but still in rhythm with them,' Rick instructed. 'Let's go back to the basic harmonies and we'll add the main melody in later.' He raised his arms to conduct, and the group stilled.

Serena rested her bottom on the edge of the registration desk and enjoyed the sound as the group started the intro to 'Oh, Happy Day'.

She was just starting to hum the missing melody when, from behind her, another voice broke in. It was rich and sweet, easily able to reach both high and low notes. Serena swung her head round and stared. One by one the choir members stopped singing until that one voice filled the low-ceilinged room and reverberated off the walls.

Her voice was hoarse with amazement when she finally

managed to speak. 'Max! Where on earth did you learn to sing like that?'

Max went suddenly silent and his face reddened. He shrugged and returned to sweeping the biscuit crumbs off the floor. She walked over to the coffee bar where Jake stood, just staring at his number-one fan.

Make that his number-two fan.

'Are you sure I can't get you anything, Dad? A cup of tea? Coffee?'

'No, I'm fine. I just want to sit out here and enjoy the fresh air for a bit.'

Serena hovered behind the garden seat and stared at her father. He'd been back for two days and she was really worried. She was used to extremes from him. This wasn't normal. He was too quiet, too steady.

'Go on, petal. You've got things to do,' he said, without turning to look at her.

She shuffled her way back through the dew-soaked grass and into the house. After making her way up to the study, she turned on the computer and checked her e-mail, all the while resisting the desire to switch to her internet browser and click the link to the Jacobs Associates website. It ought to have been deleted from her 'favourites' folder ages ago.

Only two weeks ago she'd shared a lunch of shrink-wrapped sandwiches with him in the playground at Ellwood Green. She hadn't had cheese after all, but a ham sandwich and a can of lemonade. They'd sat and chatted while children shrieked and ran past them. Despite Jake's dire prediction, she had enjoyed herself quite a lot.

But he wasn't returning to the community centre for the Friday night sessions now school had restarted, and she didn't know when she would see him again. Which was her own fault; she'd told him not to call her. There was no point in all the flirting if it wasn't heading anywhere—or at least not anywhere near an altar. But still, a perverse part of her was disappointed he'd respected her wishes.

A ring on the doorbell saved her itchy mouse-finger from any further temptation. She made her way down the stairs barefooted, only to find that Maggie, the housekeeper, had got there first. She stood at the front door like a guard dog, her ample figure blocking Serena's view of the visitor.

As she reached the bottom step, Maggie turned. 'There's someone here to see you. He says his name is Charles Jacobs.'

Serena's heart flipped over like a pancake.

She ran to the door and squeezed past Maggie, only to find her smile evaporating as she laid eyes on the man standing at the top of the steps. It wasn't him—almost. It was as if Jake had been fast-forwarded twenty years. Creases appeared between her brows.

Jake's father? It had to be. The likeness was striking.

'Hello,' she said, tentatively.

He smiled. Jake's heart-melting smile.

'Good afternoon, Miss Dove. Could you spare me a few moments of your time?'

'Erm…of course.' Behind her, she was aware of Maggie standing down from bodyguard duty and marching back to her vacuuming.

'Please, come in.' She opened the door wide and gave him plenty of space to come into the hall, then waited until he was well clear before she shut it again. He followed so close behind her on the way to the sitting room she was tempted to pick up speed.

She chose an armchair, feeling the need for her own space, and indicated that he should take a seat on the generous sofa. He eased himself onto the wide cushions, stretched his arms along the back and hooked his right foot across his other knee.

The smile came again. She sat up slightly in her chair and studied him. It was *similar* to Jake's smile, but it wasn't the same—something was missing.

'I'm afraid I don't really understand why you are here, Mr Jacobs. Can I help you somehow?'

He slouched even further into the sofa, and took his time looking around the room.

'Oh, yes. I think you can help me. Most definitely.'

Serena's heart began to pick up speed. 'Is there something the matter with Jake?' She started to rise, but sat back down abruptly when he shook his head, hand raised. His eyes gleamed. Her level of distress seemed to please him.

'No. Jake is fine. And he'll continue to be—with your help.'

'I don't understand.'

Charles Jacobs leaned forward, his smile knowing and self-satisfied.

'I know you've been seeing my son, Serena. And I think some of the gossip mags would pay well for that little titbit. However, I could forget about that kind of windfall with the proper…incentive.'

Serena laughed. 'I'm sorry, but you're wasting your time. Jake and I went out for a while, but we broke up months ago. Hardly front-page news. Your threat doesn't carry any weight, Mr Jacobs.' She rose from her seat and held the sitting room door wide. 'I think it's time you left.'

He didn't even make a pretence of getting up. 'Not so fast. If it doesn't matter to you, it might matter to Jake.'

'I can't see how—'

'Especially if I get a bit chatty and start to recount stories from his childhood. I don't think his titled clients would appreciate learning of his arrest for robbery and drug possession, do you?'

She let the door swing closed.

Drugs? Robbery!

'I don't believe it. Jake would never steal. He's just not like that.'

'Ah, well, I'm sure Jake has told you all about that little *misunderstanding*.'

Of course he hadn't! There was so much of himself he kept under wraps, so much he refused to share with her.

'But there are the records, you see. Someone could get the wrong idea. You know what they say about mud sticking, don't you? Who knows what damage a rumour like that could do?'

The man was pond scum! Ready to sell his own son for a quick buck.

However, she couldn't ignore him. That kind of information *could* hurt Jake's career, and the last thing she wanted was to see him suffer. Blood pounded in her temples.

Could she? Could she give in to him and make this all go away for Jake? His firm was everything to him. He'd built a career and a reputation, despite his father's actions. She couldn't let this slimy little man destroy all of that with one idle rumour, it just wasn't fair.

'How much *reimbursement* would you need?'

'Twenty grand.'

She blinked. He was slick, but he hadn't done his homework. He could have asked for a lot more. It would be easy. She was a joint signatory on several of the bank accounts, and her father would begrudge her nothing.

She walked to the window and stared outside. Dad was sitting on the bench where she'd left him. Could she really take his money and give it to Charles Jacobs? A pang of guilt speared her.

Jacob's beady eyes had been on her the whole time; she knew that without looking. Now she turned to meet his gaze. Eyes that same boundless blue, but lacking in any warmth or humanity.

He smiled, and her stomach churned.

'It's not much to ask for the man you love.'

She started. *The man she loved.* Heat rose in her cheeks.

'I told you. We're not seeing each other any more.'

It was too late. He knew. Betrayed by the fear in her eyes.

Her suspicion was confirmed when he settled himself on the couch again, a satisfied smirk on his face. He had her exactly where he wanted her.

'I presume you'll want cash? It'll take me a day or so to make the necessary arrangements.'

'Clever girl! I knew we'd get on famously.'

'How will I contact you?'

'I'll give you my mobile number.' He pulled a crumpled scrap of paper out of his coat pocket. 'Pen?'

Serena opened a drawer and threw a ballpoint in his direction. She wasn't going to get any closer than absolutely necessary. He scribbled something on the back of what looked like a bus ticket and crossed the room to hand it to her.

She took the ticket and stuffed it in her pocket, still keeping her eyes on him. He was too close, but her back was against the window and there was nowhere else to go.

He reached for a strand of her hair and let it slide between his thumb and forefinger. 'My son is a fool. He should never have let you go.' His breath warmed her cheek. Stale beer and dog-ends. She crunched her neck back in an effort to keep as much distance between them as possible.

'Never mind. We're like peas in a pod, me and Charlie. How about trading him in for an older, vintage model?'

She turned her head and his lips made contact with her cheek, leaving a slimy trail. While surprise had him at a disadvantage, she shoved him away with every ounce of strength at her disposal and rounded the sofa. It was a hell of a lot safer with a barrier between them.

She was so furious her voice cracked when she shrieked

at him. 'Get out! You are *nothing* like Jake! Nothing! He's everything that you're not—good and kind and honest.'

'That's his reputation *now*! Wait until I've finished with him. It'll be the messiest trial by media you've ever seen.' He paused and allowed himself a sneer. 'If you love him, you'll pay. It doesn't matter what you think of me. Take it or leave it. It's that simple.'

'I'll leave it.'

'What?'

Under any other circumstances the look of pure bewilderment on his face would have made her howl with laughter.

'I said, I'll leave it, thank you very much.' Then she did laugh, but it was short and hollow. 'You know what? I bet if you tried this on Jake he'd send you packing.'

The steely glint in his eye told her she'd hit the bullseye.

'Well, I'm not playing your little game either, *Mister* Jacobs. So you can take your pathetic little blackmail scam and try it on someone—'

He lunged towards her, and everything seemed to slow to half-speed. She had a split second to consider the fact she'd pushed him too far before he made another grab at her. The sofa didn't stop him after all, as it turned out. She almost got away, but he caught the end of the crushed velvet scarf that was looped around her neck and pulled it tight, arresting both her escape and her air supply.

She stumbled, and the side of her face crashed against a bookcase, sending shooting pains across her cheekbone. The fingers of his free hand tangled in her hair and he yanked her back towards him. Her roots screamed for mercy.

As he swung her round to face him all that crossed her mind was how odd it was that a face blessed with good looks and bone structure could contort itself into such a picture of hatred. She was still staring at him, coughing and struggling for breath, when the door crashed open.

Jacobs almost dropped her in surprise.

'Get your hands off my daughter or I'll rip your head off!'

Never had she been so glad that her dad was a solid-set man with a glint of danger in his eyes. It was just that hard edge that had kept the band popular for so long.

The hands that had been merciless a few seconds ago now pushed her away. He might be tough with a woman half his size, but it was a different matter when he was faced with her father, the pit-bull.

She hardly noticed him scuttle from the room. All she could take in was her father. Suddenly he seemed bigger and stronger, just like when she was little and he had ruled the world.

They clung to each other for a few minutes. He held her tight and stroked her hair away from her face, the way he'd used to, and looked down at her with fierce protectiveness.

Her lips crumpled into a smile.

'Thanks, Dad.'

'Any time, petal.'

He had to know.

If his own father was going to sell him to the highest bidder then he had a right to be forewarned. She stared at the doorbell and, not for the first time that night, wondered if she'd made the right decision.

Fine time to discover a belated need to stand up for herself! Her moment of victory might send Jake's career into a nosedive. The tug of anxiety in her stomach was double-edged. There was the churning anticipation of the pain her confession might cause Jake, but also the more urgent, dragging need just to see him again, the sheer indulgence of being close to him.

She jammed her thumb on the button before she could think herself into chickening out.

CHAPTER EIGHT

JAKE looked up from the mound of papers on his desk. He'd been adding a column of figures in his head, and was only vaguely aware of a foreign noise. Although the flat was silent again, the subliminal memory of the door buzzer still hummed in his ears. The old leather chair creaked as he stood up.

He didn't need to ask his visitor's identity when he reached the intercom. A huge pair of searching eyes looked up at him, their beauty undiluted by the grainy black and white picture from the CCTV monitor.

The figures he'd been holding in his memory fluttered away.

She didn't speak. She didn't need to. Her eyes said it all. *Let me in.*

But he knew that opening the door meant more than giving her entry to his home. Two whole weeks he'd managed. Two whole weeks of ignoring the phone number he kept doodling in the margins of his spreadsheets. Not only was he putting himself in danger by letting her into his life again—letting her go had hurt too much to repeat the experience—but he was putting her happiness at risk too. She'd made that quite clear. And he wouldn't do anything to make her unhappy.

He waited a moment or two before he pressed the buzzer

with an unsteady finger. When she turned the corner at the top of the stairs he was waiting for her at the threshold.

There were no hellos. They both knew they were way beyond small talk, were communicating with each other on a much deeper, more instinctive level. She spoke to a part of him that hid behind the logic and iron defences. For the first time in years he wished he were different, capable of saying *I do*.

He didn't want to break the silence. The air was charged with whatever was pulsing between them, and words would only break the bubble.

Serena looked away, and he knew she was ready with a pin.

'We need to talk, Jake.'

He smiled and reached for her hand, reluctant to make his mouth form an answer. Then she looked back at him and he knew there was no putting it off.

'Must we?'

She let out a breath and her shoulders drooped. 'You're not going to be smiling like that when you've heard what I've got to say.'

Her fingers slid out from between his and she folded her arms across her front.

'I'm listening,' he said, and motioned for her to go inside. She went through to the lounge and perched on the edge of an armchair without taking her coat off.

The eyes looked at him, pleading him to understand. Begging for forgiveness?

What on earth could she have to confess to? Only one horrible thought jeered inside his head. She'd found someone. The husband-hunt was over. His stomach knotted at the thought, which was very hypocritical of it, considering he had declined the role. He could hardly gripe if she'd found a more suitable candidate.

But the fact that she was here at all acknowledged something...unfinished between them.

She leaned forward slightly, her hair falling in dark sheets either side of her face.

'I had a visit from your father today.'

'*My* father?'

'Yes. Charles Jacobs the elder. Not a very uplifting experience.' Her hand shook as she tucked her hair behind her ear. 'I think I may have made the most awful mistake.'

A smudge of deep pink lay at the point where her temple met her cheekbone. Immediately he was across the room, crouching in front of her. His fingers gently explored the bruise and raised area beneath. She flinched.

Blood began to pound so hard in his head he could barely see straight.

'Did he...did my father do this?'

She nodded, and her eyes glistened. 'I'm sorry.'

In one swift movement he launched himself to his feet. 'God, that man is a piece of work!' Long strides propelled him around the room. Where he was going was anyone's guess. He just needed to move.

'See—this is what he does. It's his MO. He acts like an animal, then makes you feel it's *your* fault. He twists it all around so you're not sure of your own motives any more. You start to doubt yourself... He's poison.'

He managed to slow himself down enough to sit on the edge of the coffee table opposite her. His knees brushed hers.

'Nothing about this is your fault! *Nothing*. Look at me.' He waited while she edged her eyes to meet his gaze. His voice crept into a whisper. 'It's not your fault—got it?' She nodded, but his words didn't seem to have soothed her at all. 'I knew he could be violent, but I never dreamed... How could I have known he would take it out on you? He didn't give any indication...'

Before he knew it, he was striding again.

'Actually, I think I earned this little trophy all on my own,' she said quietly. 'It was nothing to do with you. Not really.'

He stopped to look at her, but she was staring at the grain on the wood floor.

She didn't get it. He could hardly expect her to. It had taken him years to unravel his father's lies and see them for what they really were. The man was a master manipulator. It was how he earned his living, after all. He sucked dry anyone unlucky enough to cross his path, then moved on to the next victim.

When he spoke, although his voice was low and emotionless, the words scared him. 'I could kill him.'

Never before had he felt such pure hate. He'd thought he'd scraped that barrel well and truly dry. But, true to form, his father could always sink lower, and he realised there were depths to hatred he had never imagined.

'I'm going to find him and I'm going to… I don't know what I'll do, but he's not getting away with this.'

Where was his coat?

He ran into the kitchen and grabbed it off one of the high-backed stools, only vaguely aware of the sound of Serena's heels coming closer. When he turned she was right behind him.

'You stay here,' he ordered. 'He won't dare come here. I don't know when I'll be back.' He swung his coat on.

Too many words. He was wasting time. He just had to get out through that door and do something. His father was a creature of habit. The events of the last few weeks confirmed the old leopard's spots were still firmly in the same place. He had favourite pubs and betting shops. It wouldn't take long.

Serena was still keeping up with him as he neared the front door.

'Jake, you can't… Will you just…?' She gripped his sleeve and gave it a violent tug.

'Don't worry,' he said, and gave her a kiss on the forehead. 'I won't let him touch you again.'

'Jake! Stop! Listen to me!'

He stopped halfway through the door. Something in her voice demanded he obey.

Her breath was coming in gasps. She inhaled deeply, then continued. 'I haven't told you what I came here to tell you! If you go off half-cocked now it will only make things worse!' Her eyes pleaded with him. He was a total sucker for that look. 'Come back inside and sit down, and let me explain everything. Please?'

She was right. He hadn't let her talk. It was just such a stab in the gut to think of anyone hurting her. The fact that it was his flesh and blood that had done the damage just twisted the knife further. He let her pull him back into the flat.

Now he'd capitulated, all the fight went out of her. She closed her eyes and massaged the lids by dragging the flat of her hand across each eye.

'Get us a drink, and let's discuss this like rational human beings.'

When he appeared from the kitchen, a glass of red wine in each hand, she had taken off her coat and was right in one corner of the three-seater sofa, back straight, ankles crossed. She took the wine when he offered it, and placed on the coffee table in front of her without tasting it.

He opened his mouth, but she silenced him with a look.

'Just let me talk. It won't take long.'

He nodded, then sat down on the opposite end of the sofa and turned to face her. She didn't look at him, but straight ahead.

'I came to warn you that your father is ready to ruin your career. He came to ask for money, to buy his silence.'

'About us? I told him we were—'

'Jake!' Now she turned to look at him.

'Sorry. Listening.'

'Not about us. About you, and something that happened when you were younger.' She picked at a nail. 'Something to do with the police.'

It was so hard to keep quiet. He was practically bursting to explain. Surely she didn't believe…?

'He said it would hurt your business if word got out. I almost paid him. But then I…well, I just couldn't. So now he's going to go to the press and see what he can get off them. I'm so sorry. I should have stopped him.' She looked up at him. 'You can talk now. If you want.'

Too many sentences battled to be the first one out of his mouth. He took a large gulp of wine to sluice the words away. She looked firmly planted in her seat, but he could tell she was walking a tightrope.

'It's okay. I know what he's like. He came to me first and I told him to get lost.' He paused and watched as she crossed, then recrossed her legs. 'I would be more upset if you had given in to him.'

'But your clients! Won't they disapprove?'

'It's possible, but it's not as bad as Dad made it sound. He's clever—a good enough con-artist to know you should always build a lie on a grain of truth. Yes, I was arrested at age fifteen for burglary. But I was very quickly released when, despite my protestations of guilt, they decided I was covering for someone else.' He leaned back in the sofa and stretched one arm along the back. 'What I don't understand is why my father went to you at all.'

Finally, she took interest in her wine glass. When she could delay it no longer she spoke. 'I think he was trying his luck at first. Then he realised there was some leverage to be had in the situation.'

'But we aren't even an item any more. Not officially,' he said, rather too quickly. 'I think we're something. I'm just not sure what.'

At least she looked relieved at that. There was hope yet.

'I think your father realised I still…' Half of him wanted her to say it; the other was half terrified she would. '…care for you.'

They sat and sipped their wine, neither knowing what to say.

'Serena?'

Her face flushed, and he knew without a shadow of a doubt that her heart had to be thudding like his. He shifted along the sofa again. Now he was close enough to smell her perfume.

'What if I told you I've missed you?'

He was coming closer. Her lips tingled in anticipation. Kissing him would be a really bad idea. It would only be harder to walk away again. But she couldn't move—didn't want to. Her hands reached up and cupped his face, making sure he closed the distance, leaving nothing to chance.

His lips were warm and soft and intoxicating. She responded with a hunger that had jump-started itself out of nowhere.

Just for a moment it didn't matter that this was the worst idea in the world, that it would only make things messy and complicated. She needed him. Needed this. Needed his lips exploring hers, craved his touch. Inside she smiled, triumphant in the knowledge that he was just as trapped. The fact they were both cursed with this peculiar insanity only bonded them closer together.

This was her last chance. She might never have him in her arms again, yet her love for him was spiralling like a cyclone out of control. She couldn't tell him how she felt, but she could show him. She would pour every ounce of her heart into this one kiss as her parting gift. Maybe somewhere, in the sections of his heart he had cordoned off, he would keep it, and one day know the treasure she had offered him.

So, as their lips continued to brush and tease, she explored the planes of his face with her fingers, ran her hands over his neck and chest, and tried to imprint every last contour in the nerve-endings so she would never forget.

He groaned, a sound from deep within his chest, and dragged her even closer to him. Their arms and legs tangled, and she continued her memory map of him by adding the toned muscles of his shoulders and back to her collection.

Whatever she was doing, it was spurring him on to even greater levels of need. Every cell in her body burst into flame. To make love to him would be the sweetest madness. She was almost tempted to throw herself off the cliff. But the wreckage of the morning after would be unbearable, knowing she would not have him for ever. She would never survive to find anyone else. There would be no hope of mending her broken heart in a few years and moving on.

As his mouth left hers to paint tiny kisses all over her face, she thought her heart would burst with the bittersweet sensation.

Don't punish me for this! I can go just a little bit crazy before self-preservation kicks in and I have to leave.

Then he stopped, so still she could feel his heart beating against her own ribcage.

She opened her eyes and focused on him. His pupils were so large they almost obliterated the brilliant blue of the irises. The expression he wore was—what? Surprise? No, guilt. He looked as if he'd just kicked a puppy. His tongue darted over his lip, tasting something. He suddenly looked ten years younger, confused and defensive.

'You're crying,' he said.

She pressed the pads of her fingers to her cheek and discovered he was right.

Without realising it she had broken the spell. Part of her screamed that it was too soon, she wanted more, one more taste of him. But there would always be that hunger for *one more*. Perhaps it was better this way.

She unhooked her leg from over his and slid away from him, tucked herself back into the corner of the sofa. He let her go, sat up himself, and ran a hand to smooth his tousled hair. Her fingers ached to rake through it and mess it up again.

'All this doesn't change anything, does it?' he said, his voice blank. 'We still want different things out of life. You want your Mr Perfect to have your two point four kids with. I'm not him. I'm not even close.'

She could agree. She could straighten her hair, put on her coat, smile nicely and tell him it had all been a terrible mistake. Then months from now, if they met, they would kiss each other on the cheek and pretend it didn't matter, pretend they hadn't thrown away their chance of happiness.

She couldn't do it. Tomorrow she might hide her head under the pillow and groan with mortification about what she was going to say, but tonight she didn't care. She had to understand.

'I think you're perfect for me.'

He pressed a finger against her lips. 'Don't.'

Her hand closed over his and she drew it into her lap.

'I'm not perfect, Serena. I told you before. You see what you want to see.'

She shook her head. 'No. At the beginning that was true. You fitted the picture of my identikit husband closely enough for me not to delve deeper—you were right about that then, but not now. Over the last few weeks I've seen the real you I'd only had a hint of before. The Jake who takes time to stick with an awkward kid that everyone else has written off. The Jake who takes care of his little sister and is always there for her. A Jake who is full of imagination, passion and patience.' Her voice caught in her throat and came out husky. 'The man who would have stopped at nothing a few minutes ago to defend my honour. The man who has captured my heart completely.'

Looking him in the eye right now was the bravest thing she had ever done.

'I love you, Jake.'

He didn't breathe out for a full ten seconds.

There. She'd done it. This was as low as she could go. The ground could go ahead and do its swallowing.

His voice was low and croaky. 'And I...haven't felt this way for a long time.'

Something inside her swelled. Maybe it wasn't as hopeless as she'd thought. Then he continued, and her hopes came crashing down.

'But I'm no good at long-term relationships. I'm a disaster waiting to happen.'

'That's the second time you've said something like that. Tell me about her, Jake?'

'More wine first.' He went to fetch the bottle from the kitchen, and when he reappeared she knew from his face it had just been an excuse so he could batten down the hatches, get his emotions firmly back under control. The way his jaw clenched told her he was having less success than he'd hoped.

Good.

He topped up both their glasses and sat down, keeping at least three feet between them.

'Her name was Chantelle. Her family moved onto the estate when I was seventeen. She was the prettiest girl I had ever seen. It took me two years to pluck up the courage to ask her out. I was sure she'd say no—but she didn't. A year later I asked her to marry me. I was sure she'd say no to that too, but she surprised me again. I couldn't have been happier.'

Knives were carving great chunks out of Serena as she heard this, but she had to know.

'So what happened?'

He refused to look back at her, and she watched his profile as he continued, brows heavy, holding his glass so tight between both hands she thought it might shatter.

'As the wedding date drew closer I started to feel differently. My friends told me it was just the wedding jitters, but I knew it was more than that. Suddenly she seemed demanding and needy, but that wasn't the case, really. She could feel me pulling away and she was scared. The closer we got to for ever, the worse it got.'

'Please tell me you didn't jilt her at the altar.'

'No. We broke up two months before the wedding. I was twenty-one; she was nineteen. Everyone said we were just too young.'

He looked over at her, pain etched in his eyes.

'I knew it was me. I couldn't give her the support and love she deserved. In the end, she couldn't take what she called my "emotional unavailability" any more, so she ended it.'

He drained his glass and sloshed more wine in to fill the space.

'And the terrible thing was, as much as I loved her, I was royally relieved.' He gave her a wry smile. 'It seems, much as I like to kid myself it's not true, I've got some of the old man's genes after all.'

'And there hasn't been anyone since?'

'Well, I've dated, but all my energy has gone into the business. I'm happy with the way things are. I don't want to change.'

Liar. The way he'd agonised over Chantelle told her he *did* care. He just pretended he didn't because it was easier.

'So that's where I am now. Which leaves us wanting different things. I can't promise you all my tomorrows.'

'Couldn't you promise me even one?'

'Of course!' He rammed his glass down on the table. 'But

it's all or nothing with you, isn't it? I can't stop thinking about you, Serena. I think we could be good together. It could last for quite a while, if we give it a chance.'

Oh, goody!

Jake got up and walked to the window. Serena slouched against the arm of the sofa and stared at the wood grain on the highly polished coffee table.

His voice was so low she could barely hear it. 'Move in with me.'

'Pardon?'

Jake turned to face her. The scariest thing was that the expression on his face was totally serious.

'Come and live with me, Serena. I want more than dinners and trips to the opera. I want to do the everyday things with you: watch TV together, cook a meal, tell each other how our days have been over dinner.' He paused. 'I want to share my life with you.'

'For now.'

'Yes, for now. It's the best I can offer.'

It made her ache to see how hard he was trying. She knew this was a huge step for him, but the thought terrified her.

'I can't live with that level of uncertainty—knowing one day you might decide you're tired of me and I'll come home to find my stuff in boxes on the landing and the locks changed.'

Jake looked ready to hurl his glass across the room. 'I would *never* do that to you.'

Serena scrunched up her face with her hands.

'I know, I know. I'm sorry, that came out all wrong. What I'm trying to say is that I don't want to waste time on a relationship that's not going to last. I would just feel like I was marking time until it all fell apart.'

'Right now, I can't ever imagine that happening.'

'But you can't promise it won't.'

'Even if I did, it might not change anything. Look at the divorce rate. There are no guarantees, even with a marriage licence.'

'But at least those people start out knowing they want the same thing, Jake. I want a family—a real family—children and dogs and a house that's always a little bit messy.' She looked round the room at the spotless furnishings. Not a coffee ring or a speck of dust in sight. 'I don't want to live in a slick city apartment while my biological clock ticks away my chance of all that. You don't want children, do you?'

He shook his head.

'That's a deal-breaker for me, Jake. I desperately want a family, and if we're just living together and "seeing how it goes" it's not enough. Children deserve a mum and a dad who are going to be there for them. You of all people should know about that.'

Jake was very quiet, just looking at her. The pained expression on his face told her this was hurting him just as much as it was hurting her. She thought he was going to say something, but the words never came. Probably because there was nothing to say. No way past this. No future for them.

She bowed her head and let the tears that had welled up fall into her lap. Jake was across the room in a second, hauling her into his arms, kissing her neck and face. It took all the effort she had to wrench herself away from him.

She dug her hands into the corners of her eyes and scrubbed away the tears. 'No, Jake. It's no use. We'd always be pulling in opposite directions.'

'In other words, I'm a waste of your time.'

Good. Anger was good. If he kept kissing her like that she'd forget why she had to be strong. And if she wanted babies she needed to be strong. She was going to give them all the stability and comfort she never had.

Now she understood. She knew Jake was not the man to give that to her. He was afraid, too scared of being like his no-good father to give love a real chance. Hedging his bets, as he wanted to, wasn't real love. It was like riding a bike with stabilisers for ever because you were too petrified you wouldn't whiz down the path like the other kids.

She got up, put on her coat and started buttoning it up.

'I think you're right. We *are* wasting each other's time. Tragic, but true.'

Her disobedient fingers finally managed the last button.

'What are you going to do about your father?'

He walked back over to the French doors and stared out the glass. 'I don't know. I expect I'll talk to the police. He can't go around demanding money from people like that. It's time I stopped pretending he didn't exist and dealt with him.'

She walked over to him and kissed his shoulder. He wasn't going to turn around from looking out of the window. She knew that.

'Goodbye, Jake. I'll never forget you.'

Serena's key twisted in the lock and she pushed the door open.

Silence.

No lights were on. She fumbled for the switch in the hall and dropped her handbag on the floor.

'Dad?'

Maggie had gone to St Albans to visit her son, but someone should be here. Dad should be here. She shrugged off her coat and left it in a heap on the floor, then ran down to the kitchen. A tap dripped in the dark. The kettle was cold.

She took the stairs two at a time and raced to his bedroom, her heart hammering.

Empty.

That was when she really started to panic. She slumped onto

the bed and picked up one of his discarded shirts and hugged it.

What *was* it with the men in her life?

She ran back out onto the landing and into every room, turning the lights on as she went. Soon the whole house was ablaze, with chandeliers and spotlights alike.

Finally she trudged down the stairs and sank down, her bottom on the last step.

Dad could be anywhere when he was on a drinking spree. She might not see him for days. There were no tears left to cry. She'd used up her supply on the way home from Jake's. The taxi driver must have thought she was a nutcase! Dad was her only point of stability now, and a pretty shaky one at that.

Anger flooded through her. She'd had such hopes for her father when he'd come home. If he self-destructed this time, she knew there would be no coming back. In her gut, she knew it had been his last chance.

Eventually, her abandoned coat annoyed her enough for her to go and pick it up and sling it over a chair. She threw off her boots and padded down the corridor to the kitchen in her stockinged feet.

As she reached the bottom of the narrow staircase that led to the basement kitchen, she stopped. Something was out of place. A glow of orange light spilled from under a door at the bottom of the stairs. A doorway so little used in recent years she'd almost forgotten it was there.

Gingerly, she pushed the door with her fingertips and it swung open. Their basement was huge. The kitchen occupied the back part that led to the garden, but more than half the area was taken up with her dad's recording studio. She pushed open a second sound-proofed door and stopped in her tracks.

Her father was sitting on a stool in the middle of the room, guitar perched on his knee. Every now and then he stopped playing and scribbled something in a notebook balanced on the edge of the baby grand.

He was writing again?

He hadn't written a song in years.

Now the tears came, hot and fast. She should have had more faith, should have believed a little harder.

Dad didn't even see her. He was facing away from her and a pair of headphones covered his ears. She dragged her hands across her face to wipe away the tears. She could see from his three-quarter profile that he was smiling.

A tiny laugh gurgled up her throat and came out as a hiccup. Then she crept back the way she had come, her shoeless feet making no sound on the rich carpet.

CHAPTER NINE

THERE was no way to sit on the metal bench to make it comfortable, especially after forty minutes. Jake traced one of the holes punched in the seat with the tip of his finger. The dark blue paint was flaking off and he picked at a bit.

The girl behind the desk humphed. He pulled his finger away and gave her an apologetic smile. There wasn't any hint of a thaw. Normally, in the face of such indifference, he'd use the name on the lady's name badge and schmooze a little. Only she wasn't wearing a badge, and he didn't think *Oi, you!* would go down very well.

She looked like an *Olga*. The chunky ribbed jumper of her uniform didn't do her broad physique any favours. Those shoulders wouldn't look out of place on an Olympic shot-putter.

She caught him looking at her and gave him a hard look. 'DC Carlisle will be with you shortly, sir.'

He nodded, and watched as she pulled the pencil out from behind her ear and continued scribbling in an important-looking log. His eyes swept round the small lobby, trying to find anything new of interest. The walls had been painted a soothing blue, to complement the navy of the steel bench. Even so, the foyer of Chelsea police station was the most depressing place he'd ever been.

The righteous anger of the night before had deserted him. All that was left was a creeping sense of guilt. God knew his father deserved this. He shouldn't care.

Mel had burst into tears when he'd told her his plans. She'd even confessed to seeing their father in secret. A cold feeling grew in his stomach every time he thought about how she'd learnt the hard way about Dear Old Dad. He should have done more to protect her, and he would have done if he'd have been less preoccupied. Hopefully DC Carlisle and his team would be able to recover Grandma's engagement ring when they caught up with the mongrel.

He stretched his legs and looked at the door to his right, willing someone to come and collect him. Today was a day for putting the past behind him, for ruling a line under things and getting on with his life. No more *if onlys*. He would forget her and move on to pastures new.

He sighed, pulled a pound coin out of his pocket and dumped it in the charity box on the shelf next to him. Fining himself for wayward thoughts had seemed such an inspired idea half an hour ago. Now his pocket was considerably lighter than it should have been. If he didn't kick this habit soon he was going to have to move on to notes.

However, he couldn't evict the thought of how Serena had looked last night as she'd turned to leave—quiet resignation and hopelessness. He should take the same attitude, but all he could do as he sat and waited for the detective was burn with indignation. She'd given up on him, taken all he had to offer and thrown it back at him. Being a bad risk smarted more than he cared to admit.

He was saved from further poverty by a squat man who appeared through the door.

'Mr Jacobs?'

He stood up and offered his hand. 'Detective Constable Carlisle.'

'I believe you have some information we might find useful?'

He picked up his briefcase and stood ramrod-straight. 'Yes. Yes, I do.'

'Well, if you'd like to come this way, sir?'

Jake hid a smile as DC Carlisle punched the code into the door lock. That tie was hideous. Serena would have had a fit!

Blast!

He peeled a fiver out of his wallet and stuffed it in the slot of the plastic box. Olga gave him a funny look, but he was saved from an explanation when DC Carlisle ushered him through the door to an interview room.

The door to the studio creaked as she opened it with an elbow. The tray she carried tipped at an awkward angle and tea sloshed out of the cup and into the saucer.

'Dad?'

'Over here.'

Through the long horizontal window she could see him standing at the mixing desk, messing around with sliders and buttons.

'I brought you some breakfast. You haven't been up all night, have you?'

He nodded towards the battered old sofa in the main part of the studio. A blanket was falling off one side and the dents in the cushions suggested a makeshift bed.

Hope welled in her heart as she saw him standing there, only just inhabiting the same world as her, his brain whirring with chords and lyrics.

'What have you been working on?'

He shrugged. 'Just an idea.'

'Play me a bit?'

Music flooded the room. It was soulful and atmospheric, every bit as good as his compositions of twenty years ago— better, even. There was an added depth to it.

'You know, you ought to come and help out at the music project. You've got so much experience. It seems a shame not to share it.'

Her dad made an *as if* face. Did he know how much like a teenager he looked when he did that?

'They won't want an old has-been like me around.'

'Nonsense. And I'm not just talking about music. I'm talking about life experience.'

Dad laughed so hard she thought he was going to fall off the stool he was perched on. 'I'm hardly a poster boy for good clean living.'

'But that's the point! You've made the mistakes, you know first hand what drugs and alcohol can do—and you've kicked it.'

'One day at a time, petal. Don't get ahead of yourself.'

She handed him his cup of tea. 'Just think about it, Dad. Please?'

'Okay. For you.'

'The big performance to mark the end of the project is at the end of term. It'd only be for a few weeks, Dad.'

He took a sip of his tea and smiled at her.

A sudden realisation of how lucky she was hit her like an express train. Life might have been chaotic with Dad, but she had *always* been loved. Just thinking about the contrast between her own father and Jake's made her shiver. No wonder he was so wary of commitment.

'I love you, Dad.'

An uncharacteristic sheen appeared in her father's eyes. 'I know. How could I not? You've looked out for me all this time, when I should have been looking out for you.'

'It doesn't matter.'

'It should.'

She slid her arms around his neck and squeezed him hard.

'I'll do it,' he whispered in her ear.

Just for that she rewarded him with a big kiss on the cheek. Grinning, she balanced herself against the edge of the mixing desk.

'But remember, it's only three weeks until the big performance. After that, we've got to decide what to do with the rest of our lives. We've wasted too much time.'

'Hmm.' She watched him dig a fork into the plate of scrambled eggs. 'Time to decide what I want to be when I grow up.'

'It's in here somewhere.'

Jake waited while Serena threw a purse, three pens and a pot of lip balm out of her handbag. Finally, when there was more junk on the kitchen table than in the bag, she produced a rumpled bus ticket. The innards of a woman's handbag were no longer a mystery, but still a source of fascination.

The way her fingers worked on the ticket, smoothing the wrinkles out, mesmerised him. Not so long ago those fingers had been… No.

'I really appreciate this, Serena. I know it's a little awkward…'

She looked up and smiled at him, but it was all lips and teeth. 'No problem. Really.'

He shouldn't feel the need to defend himself.

'It's going to save the police a lot of time and resources if I can set up a meeting with my father rather than them having to look for him. I'm going to phone and say I want to see him.'

She handed the ticket to him. He made very sure their fingers didn't brush.

'Do you think he'll turn up? You hardly parted on good terms last time. Won't he think it's a little fishy?'

Yup. That was the gaping hole in the plan, but what other option did he have?

'It'll be fine. We're very lucky you kept his mobile number. DC Carlisle will be chuffed. I think he's looking to get brownie points with his sergeant.'

'He's the policeman looking into the case?'

'Mmm-hmm.'

'You said they were already looking for your dad. What do they want him for?'

'Deception. Apparently Sussex police have had a warrant out for his arrest since before he went to Spain two years ago. Some scam involving lonely widows and internet dating sites, I believe.'

'I won't have to go to court, will I?'

'You don't have to press charges unless you want to. They have more than enough to detain him at Her Majesty's pleasure for the rest of the decade even without the black-mailing charges.'

'I don't know what I'm going to do. It wouldn't be very good publicity for Dad.'

Wasn't it about time she cut the apron strings?

'You need to do what *you* want.'

She started stuffing things back into the bottomless pit of her handbag—a good excuse to avoid eye contact, probably. Perhaps her dad was just a good excuse too. If she pressed charges they would keep running into each other, and every look, every bit of her body language, screamed that would never do.

He stood up too fast and bumped his knee on the table. They both ignored it.

She walked a wide path around him and led him back to the front door. He waved the bus ticket with the biro scrawl on the back. 'Thanks for this.' She didn't answer.

He knew he should have said a proper goodbye, but he needed to get away from her before he did anything stupid. If he could just reach the path before he turned around and waved, he'd be far enough away not to want to run back up the steps and pull her into his arms.

'Jake?'

Two steps to go. Don't stop. He skipped down the last steps and waited till his feet were firmly planted on the path before he turned. He'd miscalculated. The urge was as strong as ever.

'Would it help if…if *I* called your father?'

He shook his head.

'He might believe I've weakened more easily than you.'

She had a point.

'I don't want you to get involved.'

'I already am involved.' Her fingers jumped to the yellow bruise on her cheek.

'No.'

She walked down the stairs towards him. 'It would help me too, you know. If he doesn't take the bait we'll always be wondering when he'll pop up again. At least this way we've got a better chance of having some closure.'

Closure. Heaven knew he needed some of that. On more than one front.

He pulled his mobile out of his pocket. 'Let me see what DC Carlisle says.' With any luck the detective would pull the plug on her idea and he and Serena would both be spared any further agony.

Fifteen minutes later the man in question stepped out of a car and walked up to where Jake was leaning against the balustrade. He always looked crumpled, as if he'd just pulled his clothes from a tightly packed suitcase. Jake led him inside to talk to Serena.

'Hello, DC…' her eyes skittered down to his Hawaiian tie and she fought to control her lips '…Carlisle. Nice to meet you.'

If she didn't stop pacing soon she was going to wear a track in the carpet. Serena pressed her nose against the glass and tried to see if there was any hint of a grey overcoat on the horizon.

Two hours. He couldn't be much longer, could he?

She resumed her circuit of the dining room. They'd chosen to sit in here because it overlooked the front steps.

Jake was sprawled across one of the antique chairs. She wasn't sure if she dreaded or looked forward to going past him as she circled the table. Her pulse drummed that little bit faster, whatever the cause.

'Sit down. You're doing my head in.'

She kicked the back of his chair as she went past. 'Well, excuse me. Never mind this is all to help you out! Pardon me for being a bit nervous.'

'I didn't say you shouldn't be nervous.'

She yanked out a chair and plopped herself down on it with a thud. 'Better?'

'Much.'

The silence grew thick.

Jake tapped out the beat to an unknown song on the polished wood of the table. She reached over and slapped his fingers flat. He glared. Her hand curled back and she reddened.

Studying her empty cup seemed as good a diversion as any. 'I need another coffee.'

'You wouldn't be so jumpy if you hadn't pumped yourself full of caffeine.'

He was right. Of course he was right. But she couldn't just sit here waiting. Especially not alone—with him. It was driving her nuts. She gave him a high-handed look and stalked from the room. Making sure her feet clomped down the stairs to the kitchen didn't give nearly enough release. She needed to throw something, break something.

'Black with two sugars.'

The mug almost flew out of her hand.

'Don't do that!'

'What?'

'Sneak up on me.'

'I didn't sneak anywhere. You were making enough noise for the both of us.'

She banged another mug onto the counter.

'Go and ask Dad if he wants one, will you? He's through there.' She waved a hand towards the studio door and turned back towards the kettle. The thud of the door made her flinch.

Her own coffee was finished and Jake's was going cold when she relented and went looking for him. First she shoved his cup in the microwave to warm it up. Who cared if it killed all the flavour?

She found him in the studio with her dad. The pair of them were hunched over acoustic guitars, strumming away.

She plonked Jake's cup down on a shelf. His head jerked up.

'Thanks.'

'I wouldn't drink it if I were you. It probably tastes awful by now.'

Her dad's eyes darted between her and Jake. 'It was my fault, love. I asked him to stay.'

She sighed. 'Well, I suppose it's one way to pass the time. Don't let me interrupt you.' They bent their heads back over their guitars and carried on. They could have protested a little harder before they ignored her again.

If you can't beat them…

She dropped into the couch and swung her legs up. Her eyes drifted closed. All the tension had suddenly gone from her limbs. Her voice came out softly, almost dreamily. 'Jake, why don't you play Dad that thing you played me?'

Rustling from the other side of the room. Silence.

'Go on, don't be shy.'

'I'm not sure I—'

The doorbell. All three of them froze.

She rocketed to her feet, eyes wide. 'What do we do now?' Her chest was thumping. She held out a hand. Her fingers were trembling all on their own, no matter how hard she told them to stop.

'They'll need someone to make a positive ID.' Jake's mobile rang. He picked it up and punched a button. 'Yup... Okay... Will do.'

With that, he sprinted out of the room. She could tell by the rhythm of his feet on the stairs that he'd taken them two at a time. She looked at her dad. He put his guitar down and they stared at each other, ears straining.

Suddenly, she was running. She emerged into the hallway just in time to see Jake shutting the front door. He turned, a look of bemusement on his face.

'Jake? Who was it? Was it him?' Her voice was uncomfortably shrill inside her own skull.

He nodded slowly. 'They got him.'

She ran to the door and wrenched it open. Jacobs was being helped into a police car by two uniformed officers and DC Carlisle. He gave her a thumbs-up sign. She raised a hand and lifted her own thumb in slow motion. The door swung closed.

'So that's it, then? It's over.'

He didn't seem to be looking at her, at anything. 'It's over.'

'I thought it was going to be much more dramatic than that.'

'You've been watching too many cop shows.'

She slumped against the door. Hilarity seemed the only way to cope. 'I was expecting at least one "Shut it!".'

He didn't seem to have heard. So much for lightening the situation.

'Say thanks to your dad for me.' He pulled his coat off the hooks near the door. 'Bye.'

She watched him go, a sense of helplessness paralysing her limbs. 'Are you going to the performance next—?'

He was down the path, even steps carrying him away from her.

She went upstairs, collapsed on her bed, and wallowed in the sense of anticlimax.

He'd drifted out of her life. Just like that.

What she'd felt for him had deserved a momentous farewell, a mourning of what might have been. Not a half-hearted 'Bye' and a backwards wave. How could he just switch it all off like that? It made her want to scream.

She stopped outside Lewisham Theatre and cast an eye over the exterior. It had once been a lovely piece of art deco architecture—it still was under the pigeon droppings and pollution stains. She took a deep breath, smoothed her hair down and told herself she was being stupid. After all, she didn't even know if he was going to show up.

Max would be devastated if he didn't. This was what they'd all been working towards, the big gala performance to mark the end of the Youth Music Project and, hopefully, the start of enough funding to do more in the future.

She could see Cassie waving at her through the diagonal panes on the door. A hefty push and she joined the crowd milling in the foyer. Cassie gave her a peck on the cheek.

'You're looking good tonight, Cass. Finally shaken that stomach bug?'

Cassie shrugged and looked at Steve. 'Steve, tell Ren about the all the celebrities you've invited tonight.'

'Anyone I know?'

'Not apart from your dad and Daddy K.'

'Kevin.'

'Kevin, then. I don't think you've met anyone else. They're mainly homegrown celebs, doing it to raise their profile. I've got the mayor, two footballers and a model. Enough to get the front page of the local paper, I hope.'

Cassie jumped up and down and waved her arms. 'Oh, look, there's Mel!'

She needn't bother with all the flapping. Her pink hair was like a beacon. Mel spotted them in seconds and waved back.

Steve looked at his watch. 'Only five minutes until curtain-up. Let's go. I've put all the helpers and local bigwigs in a block.' He doled out tickets indiscriminately.

Cass grabbed Serena's elbow and held her back as the group set off for the circle. She waited for the others to climb a few more stairs before she hissed in her ear.

'He's here, you know.'

Suddenly her stomach became a gaping cavern and her arms turned to gooseflesh.

'Where?'

'Up there,' said Cassie, with a jerk of her head. 'He arrived ten minutes ago. I thought I should warn you.'

She squeezed Cassie's hand. 'Thanks. I don't know what I'd do without you.'

'Me neither. Now, shake a leg before we both start blubbing!'

Good point. If she was going to be within spitting distance of Jake, she might as well have her armour intact, and panda eyes definitely wouldn't pass muster.

They caught the others up and stood in a clump just inside the door to the auditorium. Steve and Cass went in search of their seats.

'Oh, look what the cat dragged in,' said Mel as Serena checked her ticket stub for the row number.

'Who?' Serena's eyes panned the circle and skidded to a halt three rows back from the balcony. 'Who is *that*, and why is she draped all over your brother?'

'That's Chantelle. She thinks she's a supermodel. Outside

of her imagination she just does a lot of catalogue work. Doesn't mean she doesn't swan around like she owns the place. Can't stand the cow.'

'Mel! I've never heard you talk like that!'

'You've never met Chantelle before.'

'And how is she so intimately acquainted with Jake?'

Mel let out a breathy hiss, as if she couldn't believe what she was just about to say. 'When Jake was younger and stupider—much stupider—he almost married her.'

She was Jake's ex-fiancée?

Serena braced herself against the doorway and took a good look at the competition. Blonde, long legs, big boobs— your basic nightmare.

Mel whispered in her ear, grateful for a bitching buddy, it seemed. 'Talk about high-maintenance! No matter what Jake says, as far as I'm concerned, she treated him like dirt, especially just before it ended. Jake, the daft boy, just kept coming back for more like a faithful little lap dog.'

Serena faced Mel and frowned. They were talking about the same Jake, right? The Jake who was always in charge, who never let a woman close enough to walk all over him? If she wanted any more proof she wasn't the woman for him, there it was.

When had he ever followed *her* around like a puppy? The only bright-eyed and over-eager one in their relationship had been her. If Jake had loved her, really loved her, he would have moved mountains, swum the deepest oceans—all those stupid things in the love songs on the radio—to be with her.

A long, slow sigh left her body. Why Chantelle hadn't basked in his adoration confounded her. What she wouldn't give to have him worship her like that, put her needs before his own.

'Why was she like that, Mel? I don't get it.'

Mel looked at the object of their discussion and her eyes

narrowed. 'She's a sneaky one, that Chantelle. I always suspected she wanted out of the relationship, but didn't want to be the one to end it. She'd talked her dad into spending a small fortune on the wedding, and he was livid when she pulled the plug.

'I think she was trying to push Jake into dumping her first, so he took all the flak. Then she could act the poor, jilted martyr.' She shook her head. 'Can't believe I didn't work out she'd turn up tonight. The whiff of free publicity alone is enough to make her crawl out of her hole.'

'Excuse me.' Someone barged past. Serena jumped out of the way and stared at her ticket stub. Row B, seat twenty-four. And Jake and the floozy were in…row C. Great. She edged along her row. What were the chances that seat twenty-four was in the far corner?

Eighteen…nineteen…

Oh, no, not… Twenty-four…slap bang in front of… She followed an endless pair of tanned legs up to the face they belonged to. Hah! Hair extensions! Fate was giving her a very small break. The thought gave her enough momentum to stretch her lips over her teeth and smile. She looked pointedly at the occupant of the seat next to the legs.

'Good evening, Jake.'

He looked as if he wanted the red velvet seat to fold up and swallow him. Serve him right.

'Evening.'

'Aren't you going to introduce me to your friend?'

Jake tugged at his shirt collar and mumbled something indecipherable.

Floozy held out a hand and regarded her with a suspicious eye. 'Chantelle. And you are…?' The defensive thrust of her chin spoilt the fairest-of-them-all effect.

'Serendipity Dove. Nice to meet you.' Her cheeks felt taut, keeping the smile in place.

Chantelle's eyes opened wide and the pout she'd been wearing transformed into a smile. 'Oh, you're…'

Serena nodded. Chantelle craned her neck and scanned the auditorium. 'Is your dad here, then?' There was something about her husky voice that rubbed Serena up the wrong way—like being caressed by a cheese grater.

'I'm sure he'll surface sooner or later. Keep your eyes peeled.'

Chantelle displayed her perfectly even, white teeth. 'We must have a chat at the interval. I expect we've got a lot in common, both being in the public eye and all.'

Mel, who had arrived next to Serena, snorted loudly.

'Oh, it's you, Melissa! I hardly recognised you now you're all grown up.' Chantelle lowered her voice to a stage whisper. 'You know, no one would ever guess you had a problem with spots when you were younger.'

Mel had that same evil glint in her eye that a Doberman got before it chewed something's leg off. Thankfully, the house lights dimmed and postponed any further insult-hurling. Serena sat down and tried to focus on what was happening on stage.

The gospel choir were the first act, and she really did try to concentrate on them. They'd improved so much. Feet were tapping and hands clapping in every direction. But not behind her. Oh, no. Chantelle leaned across to whisper into Jake's ear every few seconds. It was bad enough feeling heat creep up her neck just because his knees were only inches away, without being reminded that the floozy was the one who was actually touching him.

When the interval came, she couldn't shoot out of her seat fast enough.

Chantelle called after her. 'Good idea—get to the ladies' first. Hang on, babe. I'll come with you.'

Serena didn't bother waiting for the woman to disentangle herself from Jake. She ran to the circle bar as fast as she could and ordered a rather large gin and tonic. When the tumbler arrived she took a large sip and closed her eyes.

It wasn't long before she became aware of a couple of bodies in close proximity. *Please, no!* Relief flooded her when she opened her eyes to find Steve and Cassie standing there. She gave Cass a bear hug.

'Ren…I think you're cutting off my air supply.'

'Sorry. I'm just very glad to see a friendly face.'

Cassie's eyebrows raised.

'Long story. I'll fill you in later, but first let me get you a drink. The usual?' She turned back to the bar without waiting for an answer and waved at the barmaid. Cassie tugged her sleeve.

'Actually, I'll just have a lemonade.'

Serena spun right round and lost all hope of attracting the barmaid's attention for the next few minutes. The bar was filling up rapidly.

'Since when do you drink…?'

Cass shot a look at Steve, who was trying hard to do sheepish, but kept slipping into just plain jubilant.

'Oh, my goodness, you're not—?'

Cassie nodded.

'You *are!* That's wonderful news!'

She hugged Cassie again, making sure she didn't squeeze as hard this time. Thankfully, Steve had decided to jump in and get the drinks. He didn't see her happy mask slide as she looked over Cass's shoulder. How barren her own life seemed in comparison to her friend's.

She should be ashamed, thinking of herself at a time like this! Cassie had been her rock—the sister she'd never had. She deserved every ounce of happiness she got, and a hundredfold more.

She pulled back and took a slug of her G&T.

Cassie looked concerned. 'Are you okay? I wasn't going to tell you yet.'

'You didn't have to keep it a secret because of me.'

Cassie rubbed her arm. 'I just didn't want to rub your nose in it. I know things haven't been that great for you recently.'

There was a flash of blonde hair over Cassie's shoulder. Serena groaned. 'Don't look now! They're about to get a whole lot worse.'

She tried to hunker down and hide behind Cassie, but it was no good. Chantelle obviously had a homing device.

'There you are! We've just about got time for that chat.' She turned to Jake, who was looking the same shade of grey as his suit. 'Jay, could you get me a white wine? Ta, babes.' He was dismissed with a red-taloned hand. 'Don't mind him. He's been like that all evening. I'm not taking any notice, though. Jay and I go way back—but I'm sure you've heard all about that.'

'Not really.' She was surprised at how clear the words sounded through her gritted teeth.

'Oh. Well, we almost got hitched once upon a time, but I called it off. I don't think he ever got over it. I've heard he hasn't had a long-term relationship since.'

Chantelle gave her an assessing look. A look that told Serena she knew all about her recent relationship with Jake, and found it glaringly obvious why Jake hadn't wanted to march *her* up the aisle.

'How fascinating.'

Mel had been spot-on. Chantelle wasn't as dumb as she looked. She was staking her claim, making sure everyone knew she had first dibs on Jake, and always had. Chantelle tucked her arm into Serena's as if she were a long-lost friend and pulled her into a quiet corner, but she wasn't fooled. It was all part of the act. An act Chantelle was very good at. Every word the model uttered was another nail in the coffin, hammering her rival into place.

'It was just bad timing, really. Just before the wedding I landed a big modelling contract.'

Holding up a tin of dog food, no doubt.

'Jay was so serious back then. Always working and doing exams. He never wanted to go to the parties I was invited to. He just wanted to settle down—' she mimed a yawn '—and do boring things like get a mortgage and have babies. I wasn't about to swell up like a balloon just as my career was taking off!'

She smoothed her skin-tight top down over her hips and gave a little laugh.

'I must have spoiled him for anyone else. He didn't seem to have any problem proposing to *me*. I expect I was the love of his life.' She looked wistfully over to the crush near the bar. Jake was in there somewhere. 'People said we were too young, and I suppose they were right. But now…well, let's just say I'm older and wiser.'

A grey-suited arm thrust a glass of wine under Chantelle's nose.

'Jay, you melon! This is dry wine. I only like medium sweet—you know that.'

Jake wore a grim look as he squeezed his way back to the bar, and Serena grinned into her glass as she took another sip. Either Jake didn't care enough to remember his ex's favourite tipple, or he was making a point. Either way, he wasn't Chantelle's lap dog any more.

Right then, the cavalry arrived. Cassie and Steve found them, and Steve made the mistake of asking Chantelle if he recognised her from somewhere. Pretty soon she'd launched into a monologue on all the designers she'd worked with, and how many minor-league pop stars she'd left broken-hearted.

Serena searched the sea of heads near the bar and found Jake's within seconds. Maybe the exact shade of his hair had stuck in her memory. It was like spotting the right jigsaw piece and knowing it was the one that was going to fit. She watched him work his way towards their group, diverting her eyes at the last moment, so he wouldn't know she'd been watching him.

Chantelle accepted the glass he offered her and took a gulp or two. 'Oh, good—that's much better!'

Jake elbowed his way round to stand at Serena's other side and whispered in her ear. 'This isn't what it—'

She knocked back the gin and tonic and slammed the glass down on a table. 'Well, I must get back.'

Chantelle's mouth turned down. 'Must you? Well, we'll have to go for a drink afterwards. Maybe after I've met your dad?'

'He's rather busy tonight.'

'Oh, we just want to say hi—don't we, Jay?'

Jay grunted.

Serena fled before she had to face any more. No way was that woman getting within twenty feet of her dad. Jake would be dropped like a hot brick and she'd be calling her *stepmummy* before you could say collagen injection!

Over my dead body. Or hers.

She sat in her seat, arms folded, shoulders hunched, for the second half of the programme. If Chantelle kicked the back of her chair one more time…

She hardly heard a note of the performance. When she actually managed to wrench her attention from the two seats behind her, the thought of watching from the sidelines while Steve and Cassie built their family shredded her like a knife. She rubbed her forehead. Her friends had a future full of love and sunshine while her own was as bright as a bucket of Thames mud.

Perhaps she should stop planning her tomorrows like a military campaign. Do what Cassie had done. Perhaps she shouldn't hunt love down, but let it find her instead. But she was scared to let go and go with the flow. What if she just ended up washed out to sea—alone?

Grabbing on to any sign of security had seemed a much better plan, but she realised now it wasn't working. The things she grasped for always slipped through her fingers anyway.

Her dad, Max, and a couple of keyboard players filed onto the stage. She'd heard them rehearse all week, and it was going to bring the house down. The song was a fusion of rock guitar and hip hop, with Max's smooth vocal over the top. If that boy didn't have a recording contract in the next six months she'd eat her crocheted hat. Funny how all thoughts led back to Jake.

Chantelle's stilettos made jarring contact with the back of her seat again. She was living her worst nightmare. If the immediate torture of seeing the man she loved being pursued by another woman wasn't bad enough, her long-term plans for her personal life were looking even more bleak. She had no love-life, no husband, no babies—no future.

Of course she could change the *no love-life* part if she moved in with Jake, but that meant giving up her dreams. In the end she'd be back at square one, and maybe too old to find someone else who wanted to have children with her.

She sat very still. What if she got pregnant—with Jake's baby? Even if the relationship didn't last, she'd still have the baby. She looked from side to side, just to make sure no one could tell what she was thinking.

Now, this shows just how desperate I'm getting! Wake up, Serena!

She couldn't do that to him. Jake would want to do the right thing. She'd have him trapped and he would hate her for it eventually. She wanted his heart and soul, not just a family car in the garage and his and hers toothbrushes in the bathroom. The clamour of the auditorium vanished. Her chest rose and fell. Her heart thudded.

She wanted Jake, heart and soul.

The question was: what was she prepared to sacrifice to get him?

CHAPTER TEN

THE SWING DOOR closed and hit her on the bottom. She moved to one side and leant back against the smooth plaster wall. The cool air of the stairwell was delicious. Out here, away from the others, it was easier to see things for what they really were.

Chantelle wasn't any competition really. She was hardly a blip on the radar. Even if she wanted to cast herself in the role of *femme fatale*, it was obvious Jake wasn't interested

Serena knew Jake was *her* man. For now.

But Chantelle was a warning. One day a woman who was a more serious threat might be hanging on his arm, and Serena's chance would be gone. It was time to stuff her fears into the bottom of her handbag and seize the moment.

A few more deep breaths and she was ready to head down the stairs to the dressing rooms. Once in the warren-like basement, she set about tracking down her father. Benny's familiar bulk was placed outside dressing room three.

'Hey, Benny. Did you see any of the show?'

'A bit.'

'Like it?'

A nod. High praise indeed.

She knocked on the door and peeked inside. Dad was sitting on a table at one end of the room, surrounded by yabbering teenagers. They were all shouting over the top of each other, telling anyone who would listen how they'd almost tripped over, or how they'd fluffed a note. All of them had hundred-watt smiles.

She yelled to make herself heard. 'You were all brilliant!'

Raucous cheers of appreciation. She slipped into a seat next to her dad and kissed him on the cheek. 'It sounded great. The best you've played in years.'

'There's a lot to be said for being able to focus on the strings,' he said with a grin.

'Dad, I won't be going out with you and the rest of the gang after the show. There's something I've got to sort out.'

'About time too!'

She frowned.

'I might be over the hill, but I'm not blind! It's about time you and Mr Three-piece-suit sorted yourselves out.'

'Thanks, Dad.'

'Anyway, Max and I have a lot to discuss. I'm going to help him put a demo together.' Max sat on the other side of her father, doing a really bad job of being chilled about the whole idea.

'You're a star!' she mouthed to him, and he blushed. Max actually blushed!

She heard a pair of heels clacking in the corridor and her smile faded. Chantelle's radar must have gone into overdrive, being this close to a *bona fide* rock star. Serena hopped to her feet and marched to the open door.

'Benny, don't let that woman in here, or there'll be hell to pay.'

She stepped out into the corridor and pulled the door to, while Benny folded his arms and stood across the entrance. Chantelle was clomping to and fro, looking in dressing room doors. Jake stood at a distance, hands stuffed in his pockets and a forbidding look on his face.

Then he looked in her direction and they both stopped.

Bodies swarmed around them and Chantelle was forgotten. But she knew Chantelle wasn't meant for him, anyway. That was why he'd got cold feet before their wedding. It had had nothing to do with his ability to commit, that was for sure, but she suspected Jake hadn't woken up to that fact yet.

No guarantees, that was what he'd said. With love there were no sure things, only risks, and while Jake was fixated on the idea that there were no guarantees for success, there were no guarantees for failure either.

She lowered her lashes momentarily, and when she looked at him again she took all the barriers down. All her love and longing for him were there for him to see.

He swallowed, and his Adam's apple bobbed. He wanted her just as much as she wanted him. There was a sense of inevitability about all this. They had no choice, really. How stupid of them to have wasted all this time.

She wove through the moving bodies towards him and he suddenly sprang to life, forging through the crowd too. Finally they stood face to face. It was all she could do to stop herself from leaping into his arms. They were only inches apart, but she held back from touching him. Both of them knew that contact would light the touch paper, and this was neither the time nor the place.

Her voice came out all low and breathy. 'We need to talk.'

'I'll give you a lift home.'

His eyes swept over her, drinking her in. Much more was being said than just words. Body to body, man to woman.

'What about Chantelle?' she asked.

'What about her? She came here on her own. She can leave the same way. I didn't bring her. She just…latched on.'

'I know.'

They both turned and watched Chantelle trying to sweet-talk Benny. All her eyelash-flapping was getting her nowhere.

Serena and Jake smiled at each other and he reached for her hand. Her fingers slid into his and her fate was sealed, just as surely as if she'd said *I do*.

They didn't break contact until they reached Jake's car. The ride home was made in a silence thick with promise. It reminded her of the first night they'd met, when the boundaries of the universe had shrunk to fit the cabin of her dad's car.

Her heart throbbed like the engine and her nerve-endings were sensitised. Just watching him drive, watching his firm hands and strong wrists, was sending waves of pleasure crashing through her just as if he'd been touching her.

By the time the car screeched to a halt she was shaking with need.

As they climbed the steps to the front door, he caught her hand and pulled her to him. Since she was a step higher than him, they were at eye level with each other. His hands traced the contours of her cheeks, and the look in his eyes made her tremble all the more. It was more than desire, something richer and deeper, which, given enough time and room to grow, *might* turn into love.

She drank in that look.

Then her lashes lowered to her cheeks and she started to close the gap between them, slowly, savouring the ache of anticipation. Jake broke before she did, crushing her to him and claiming her lips with heady need. She clasped her hands round his neck and pulled him closer still, letting him know the heat was raging inside her too.

They stumbled up the next few steps, Jake guiding her as best he could since she was going backwards. Her back crashed into the front door, but all thoughts of keys and lights were banished from her head by the velvet of his lips upon her throat, burning kisses that set her toes alight.

She dragged her hands from the back of his head and

fumbled in her pocket. The keys felt like ice. They jangled in her shaking fingers as she tugged them free. Jake refused to let her go when she turned to slide her key into the lock. His hands flew under her coat, caressing her through the clingy wrap-over dress she was wearing. One hand delved under the top layer. She gasped hard and almost dropped her keyring.

Then they were falling through the front door, keys clattering somewhere on the tiles. Coats fell to the floor. Jake's weight shifted as he slammed the door closed with a foot.

He pulled away and looked at her, and her heart almost stopped. Such tenderness, such vulnerability. How did this amazing, intelligent man not understand he was nothing like his father? He was too scared to see the truth. Scared of the loss and rejection that might ensue if his fears were real. That fear had kept him a prisoner too long.

She kissed his nose, his eyelids, his brows.

I was scared too.

But she had thrown away her fears and preconceptions and jumped over the precipice. And instead of a terrifying plummet to the death, she was flying—free to love and give herself without reservation. It was glorious.

She would lead him, step by step, and if they stumbled, they stumbled, but at least they would have tried. She laced her fingers into his and led him towards the stairs. The house was as familiar to her in the dark as it was with the lights on. Jake, however, was blind. But it didn't matter. She would guide him through the darkness.

When the bedroom door clicked shut behind them, the pace slowed, as if they both knew the momentous nature of the occasion. No rushing through without enjoying the scenery. Each moment, each touch, was to be savoured, not wasted.

He stepped towards her and kissed her. His lips were so soft, so gentle, that tears sprang into her eyes. She knew she would never regret taking this path, whatever the future held. Just to experience this bliss once in a lifetime would be enough.

The tips of his fingers skimmed the contours of her body, and the string holding her dress together tensed, then fell loose. She fumbled with his tie, trembling fingers working through the knot, but she wouldn't rush. It slid free and landed by their feet.

She lowered her arms and shimmied out of her dress. It clung to her slightly as it slid down her legs and pooled at her ankles. Jake reached for her, his patience evaporating, and his long fingers slid down her back, sending ripples of delight up her spine.

Knowing she was in her underwear while he was still fully clothed only served to heighten her desire, making her feel feminine and sexy. The cotton of his shirt grazed the skin of her torso as they clung together, finally overbalancing and landing with a thump on the goose-down duvet.

Her hands were everywhere. She couldn't claim enough of him.

He was the one. She didn't care which boxes he ticked and which he didn't. He was the only one. There was no point taking her hunt any further. Any other man would only be second best. He could have her heart on his terms—no strings attached, no regrets.

She pulled his face close to hers and gave him the sweetest kiss she could deliver. 'I love you, Jake.'

He pulled her even closer, his arms so tight it felt as if he wanted to climb inside her skin. She could feel him trembling, his breathing uneven. His voice was warm in her ear. 'Oh, God, Serena, I…'

Say it! Say you love me too!

'I…can't do this.'

The air rushed cold and barren round her body as he

pushed himself away. Suddenly she felt naked rather than sexy, underwear or no underwear. This was no longer abandon; it was humiliation. She pulled her arms and legs into herself and curled into a ball.

He was panting. 'I'm sorry, so sorry. I should never have let this happen.'

Her tongue was glued to the roof of her mouth. His pity stung. She closed her eyes and turned her head away.

'I'm sorry.'

She winced.

And then he was gone, his feet thudding down the stairs, the crash of the front door, the squeal of tyres. She sat up and strained for the sound of his car until it melded with the sirens and the rumble of the city. Then she slid off the edge of the bed and collapsed onto the floor.

Her foot touched something silky. His tie. She wound it round her fingers and pulled it to her chest.

No regrets? What a fool!

She was so stupid not to have seen the signs.

Jake *could* do commitment! She'd seen evidence of it in his relationships with Mel and Max, and even Chantelle. The truth was he couldn't—no, *wouldn't*—commit to *her*, not even for a night. She had offered herself to him and he just hadn't been able to bring himself to accept her gift. He didn't want her on any terms at all.

She pulled the tie to her face. It smelled of him. The fabric was soft on her cheek, where his lips had been only moments before. She wasn't sure whether she wanted to rip it to shreds or wind it round her own neck.

She buried her face in the duvet and quivered at the thought of her humiliation.

Her eyelids were stuck together with congealed tears. She stretched them far enough for them to pop apart, lash by lash, then slithered out of bed. Her foot made contact with a soggy tissue, thrown there some time around four a.m. In fact, the whole bedroom floor was a minefield of them.

She pulled on her robe and fluffy slippers, and bent to retrieve her bra and knickers from the night before with thumb and forefinger.

She would never wear them again. Who needed a constant reminder of the most painful moment of her life? They would brush against her skin, touch the places he should have touched but had declined.

I can't do this.

She dodged the tissues and left the bedroom. A cup of tea would have to solve all her problems. She certainly didn't have any other ideas.

Back at square one.

Well, back at square minus one hundred, actually. Last time she'd been planning her happy ever after at least her heart had been in one piece, without boot-marks all over it. The weight of all she'd lost lay heavy on her chest. It hurt to breathe, to think.

Just the slightest thought of him made her stomach roll. Being lovesick had always sounded so romantic before she'd realised it involved feeling physically ill—as if she'd gone ten rounds with a bout of flu and come off the worst.

She reached the kitchen and wandered over to the sink to stare out of the window. The tint of the sky meant dawn was imminent. A few cups and plates sat in the sink. Hardly enough to bother with the dishwasher. All mind-numbing activities were heartily welcomed for the foreseeable future, so she reached for the washing-up liquid. A puff of air and three tiny bubbles were her reward.

So she stood and stared out of the window again. The bright daylight colours of the garden were hushed into hues of grey and blue and lavender. Everything seemed so peaceful, so empty. She longed to feel like that. Peaceful. Empty. Not bombarded by her senses. Colours were too bright, noises too loud, feelings too…much. She felt an overwhelming urge to let the cold grey light of the garden dampen them until they were bearable.

The instant she opened the back door the cold air hit her like a slap. It was wonderful. Anything to give her a split-second relief from her broken heart. She needed more of the same. She didn't want to think about him, to feel anything for him. She had to numb herself.

She understood her father's addictions a little better this morning. It was the only way he'd been able to cope after her mother died. Now she understood how seductive the thought of oblivion could be.

If only she could escape the gnawing pain, could forget the way his face had looked when he left.

I'm so sorry.

She found herself at the old wooden bench under the oak tree and sat down. Its weathered surface was still rough through the thin protection of her pyjamas and wrap, but she didn't care. She sat facing the blank garden wall and waited for the pre-dawn chill to freeze her heart as it had her fingertips.

The sun had turned the sky a pale apricot when her father found her shivering.

'Come back inside,' he said, reaching for her hand. 'You'll freeze to death out here.'

She let him pull her up and guide her back to the house, too drained to argue. 'It all went horribly wrong, Dad.'

'I guessed as much when I saw you sitting out there. Come on, I'll make you a bacon sandwich. I know how you love them.'

'But, Dad, you're a vegetarian. You hate—'

'It doesn't matter. It's high time I looked after *you* for a change.'

He led her into the kitchen and pulled out a chair near the sturdy table. 'You're a survivor, you know. You'll get through this.' He kissed the top of her head and then started rummaging in the cupboards for a frying pan.

Serena slumped forward and laid her cheek on the cool wood of the table. She stayed there, just watching her breath mist the surface and evaporate over and over again.

Getting through this seemed as likely to her as bungee-jumping off the top of Big Ben.

Jake checked his watch. Two-fifteen. The view from the plane window showed unrelenting grey ocean. He relaxed slightly. He was more than halfway across the Atlantic. Not a totally safe distance, but better.

He leaned his elbows on the drop-down tray and rested his face in his hands.

'Are you all right, sir?'

He twisted his head to look at the stewardess. 'Fine.'

'Air sickness?'

'Something like that. It'll pass.'

'Just press the call button if you need anything.'

'Thanks. I will.'

He pressed his thumbs into his eye sockets. He couldn't cope with the thought of how much he'd hurt her. She'd hate him, but he had to remind himself it was better this way. If she had any idea *why* he'd really done what he had, she'd keep on hoping. If she knew he loved her she'd waste her time waiting for him, instead of finding someone to give her all she needed—all she deserved.

How embarrassing. He hadn't cried since he was thirteen and Millwall had lost to West Ham. He sucked in a breath and held it, willing the stinging at the backs of his eyes to stop. He only just made it.

A few more hours and he'd be in New York. If only he'd

stayed away longer last time he wouldn't have put both of them through this. At least with an ocean between them he could hardly foul up her chances of happiness again.

The in-flight movie started—an action flick. He needed something to take his mind off Serena. But, five minutes in, things were exploding left, right and centre and all he could think about was her.

Leaving her had been the hardest thing he'd ever had to do, but he couldn't stay and see her shrivel as all her dreams died. She would be a great mother. He could imagine her covered in finger paint, giving horsey rides to a little girl with chocolate-brown eyes who could wrap her daddy round her little finger.

Rats! His cheek was wet. He might as well just shove his face in the sick bag and pretend.

Serena reached for the phone. Finally her fingers gripped it and pulled it to her ear. 'Uh-huh?'

'It's nine-thirty. Time to get out of bed!'

Cass!

'I'm not in bed.'

Silence.

'I'm sitting at my computer, fully dressed: hair combed, teeth brushed—the works.'

'Well…good. I'm glad to see you've stopped wallowing. I haven't heard from you in a fortnight.'

'I haven't been wallowing; I've been busy working on something. And, believe it or not, I'm a big girl, Cass. I can actually get out of bed on my own now and then.'

'Well, if that's the way you feel…'

'Cass, please! I know you're just looking out for me, like you've always done, but I need to stand on my own two feet. You've got to stop fussing over me!'

'I'm only trying to look after you.' Cassie sounded really hurt.

'I know! And I love you for it. But pretty soon you're going to have someone else to look after—someone even more helpless than me.'

'Only just.' Cassie tried to make a disapproving noise, but Serena could tell she was stifling a smile.

'I've spent too long hiding behind Dad, pretending I was looking after him, when really I was just playing it safe. It's time to live my life, take some risks.'

'Good for you! What sort of risks?'

'I want you to arrange another blind date for me.'

The series of muffled thumps and clunks that followed gave her a pretty good clue that Cassie had just dropped the phone. When she next spoke, she sounded breathless. 'You're kidding!'

'I'm perfectly serious.'

It took Cassie a good few seconds to stumble the next few words out. 'But…Jake…'

'…is gone, Cass. It's been a month now. I need to move on.'

'Well, if you're sure…'

'I am. Set it up for Lorenzo's.'

'Gino and Maria as back-up? Like before?'

'Too right. They'll tear strips off anyone who even looks at me funny.'

'Thanks a lot! Don't you trust my judgement?'

'Let's just say I'm covering all the bases. Look how it worked out last time.'

'Good point. Lorenzo's it is.'

'Talking of Lorenzo's, can you and Steve make it for lunch tomorrow? Dad and I have an idea we'd like to talk through with you.'

'Sounds intriguing.'

'All will be revealed tomorrow. One o'clock?'

'Sounds good. Look after yourself, sweetie.'

'You too. Bye.'

Serena put down the phone and wrote the lunch date on the calendar. Tomorrow was four weeks to the day since she'd last seen Jake. She hadn't actually marked off the days, but every time she looked at the calendar she imagined those little spiky red crosses there all the same.

She opened her internet browser and clicked on a link in her 'favourites' list. A girl could always do with a little retail therapy at a time like this. There, at the top of the list, was the link to the Jacobs Associates website. The pointer hovered over it. She clicked—and sent it to the recycle bin. A wave of sadness hit her.

It wasn't that she was over Jake. She just needed to move on with her life. Some important lessons had been learned from the whole sorry affair. The most important being that it didn't matter if the packaging wasn't conventional: love and security came in all different disguises.

She'd been so sure her upbringing had lacked stability—and sometimes it had—but she'd always been loved. She just hadn't recognised it for what it was. No more judging by appearances. And men were most definitely included in that edict.

Look at Jake. She'd picked him because he had the right look to fill her fantasy role of Mr Right—a little cardboard cut-out she could tack on to the rose-covered cottage along with the kids and two dogs.

And underneath the layers of crusty accountant she'd found a surprisingly imaginative and wonderful man, even better than her wish list—for all the good it had done her!

Asking Cassie to set her up again wasn't a sign she'd got over him. Her heart still squeezed every time she thought of him. She avoided anywhere they'd ever been together, and she couldn't find a single sensible thing to say to Mel. Just looking into his sister's blue eyes set off a whole string of memories like tiny time bombs.

No, resuming her husband-hunt was more an act of faith. Maybe one day she would find someone to love and support her. It wouldn't be like it had been with Jake. He was the love of her life—such a corny phrase, but she knew now what people meant by it. Maybe she would find someone nice to share her life with, but a little piece of her would always be reserved for Jake.

Next time she would be more prepared.

No! her heart screamed. It didn't want a *next time*.

'So, what do you think?'

Steve clapped his hands together. 'I think it's a great idea!'

Serena and her father exchanged smiles.

'What are you going to call it?' asked Cassie.

'We haven't come up with anything yet.'

Steve sat back in his chair and scratched his chin. 'What about The Phoenix Foundation? Would the other band members mind you using the name?'

Her dad shrugged. 'I'll have to ask, but I can't see it being a problem.'

'It just seems to fit, doesn't it?' Steve continued. 'The whole idea of setting up music projects in inner city areas, breathing new hope into people and places that have been written off.'

Serena squeezed her dad's hand. 'I think it's perfect. In time, once we're up and running, we'd like to offer scholarships for gifted pupils to take their music education further—or even get the music industry to give work experience placements and funded apprenticeship programmes.'

Steve smiled. 'With your contacts, Mike, nothing is impossible.'

'I'm glad you like the idea,' her dad said. 'Because we want to ask you and Cassie to be on the board of trustees. Will you do it?'

'Just try and stop me!'

Her father turned to Cassie. 'How about you?'

Cassie smiled an elfish little smile. 'When's the launch party? You've got to have a launch party! Attract a bit of publicity, get the ball rolling…'

'How about three weeks from now?' Serena said.

Cassie stared at her. 'Three weeks? That's cutting it a bit fine!'

'Not for my daughter! She's been up till all hours most nights, working on this idea. She's a human dynamo!'

'Dad can pull a few strings to get us a venue, and I'll get to work on the rest—after all, I haven't got anything else to occupy my time.'

While the others started chattering and suggesting ideas for the party, Serena sat back in her chair and folded her hands in her lap. The foundation was going to be a salvation for her—and her father too. Something positive to fill the void left by their differing personal addictions.

She waved over to the bar. 'Gino! Give us another round of Shirley Temples—and this time stick an umbrella in them. We're celebrating!'

CHAPTER ELEVEN

MERV BLUMSTEIN spoke in his nasal Brooklyn accent. 'Did you have a look at that investment opportunity I told you about? What do you think?'

'It looks like a good bet,' Jake replied.

'Are you sure?'

'As sure as I can be.' He flicked through a file. 'Nothing's a dead cert in investment terms, of course. There are no iron-clad guarantees…'

Merv coughed. 'Mr Jacobs?'

Jake snatched his focus back from the ceiling. 'Sorry. I just…remembered something similar I said to someone else.' He shook himself out of it and smiled warmly at the quizzical Mr Blumstein. 'Irrelevant, really. As I was saying, there's no way to guarantee success, but failure isn't certain either. We have to take a risk, yes, but it's a calculated risk.'

Merv nodded, but his face was pinched. For a self-made millionaire he was the most cautious man Jake had ever met. People often made that kind of money by taking chances, but not Merv. He'd probably saved every penny since he was a toddler, refusing to let anything out of his sweaty grasp.

It was daft, really. If only he'd learn to jump in and take a risk, he could be twice as rich as he was now and probably half as stressed! Life was no fun if you always played it safe…

He slapped the folder closed and handed it to his client. 'It's your money, Mr Blumstein, and you can do what you want with it. But I recommend you give this some consideration. Take the report away with you and let me know how you want to proceed when you're ready.'

Merv shook his hand and left, clutching the folder as if it contained the secrets of the ancients. Jake managed to resist wiping his hand on his trouser leg until the door was safely closed. He moved out from behind the desk and wandered to the window. It was a great *thinking* window; the view was never boring. The afternoon sun bounced off the skyscrapers, and traffic and people swarmed like multi-coloured bugs seventy floors below.

Was he really guilty of playing it safe?

He'd always thought he was so sensible in his attitude to love—keeping his distance, never getting involved. He'd told himself it was to protect the innocent, so he didn't break too many hearts. A cold feeling crept up his arms. What a load of…

He was protecting *himself*! The whole keep-'em-at-arm's-length thing had been about self-protection—until Serena, of course. He really had done what was best for her. To see her broken and dejected like his mother would have been more than he could bear. And to know that he was the one responsible for taking that generous heart and squeezing all the life out of it until it was a withered shell… He couldn't do that to her.

No guarantees…

He turned his back on the New York skyline and faced into the office. It was dingy and claustrophobic by comparison. He thought about his father. Mel had phoned only that morning to let him know when the trial date was. The image of his father as the policeman had put his hand on top of his head and guided him into the police car still hovered in his memory.

There had been no remorse, no compassion on his face, only blind rage. It was as if he believed it was undeserved, that he was not to blame. Jake just didn't get it. He'd looked at it from every angle to get inside his father's head, and still he couldn't fit the pieces of the puzzle together. He would never understand how...

A wave of nausea hit him, so powerful he almost reached for the wastebin.

He was nothing like him! Nothing like his father at all!

In appearance, maybe, but that was where it ended. Inside, they were as different as alien species. His stomach turned again. What if...what if he'd made the most terrible mistake?

He couldn't think about that now. Time was needed to digest the most recent revelation before he plumbed the even greater depths of his own foolishness.

He stabbed the button on the intercom. 'Susan?'

'Yes, Mr Jacobs?'

'Hold all my calls for the next thirty minutes. I'm...something has come up. I'm going out.'

Within five minutes his feet were in contact with the sidewalk and the multi-coloured bugs were a mass of taxis, cars and jostling people. The bustle of the Big Apple was good for crowding out any unwelcome thoughts; that was why he'd come back here.

His favourite coffee house was only just round the corner. He could buy a double espresso and read a British paper. Café Noir liked to appear cosmopolitan, and stocked a selection of international newspapers for their clientele to peruse.

Just as he was about to turn into the doorway, he stopped in his tracks. All the breath left his body.

How...?

She was hailing a cab. Sleek dark hair fell around her shoulders and her long skirt was ruffled in the light breeze. A silver bracelet danced on the wrist of her raised arm.

Then she turned, and he realised it wasn't her after all. Only a memory superimposed on a similar shell.

How many times was he going to do this? It was getting to be a weekly, if not daily, occurrence. Pretty soon he'd have to barricade himself inside his rented apartment to safeguard his sanity.

He went inside Café Noir, ordered his coffee, and grabbed a paper from the rack by the till. It was a little downmarket from what he usually read, but it was the best he could lay his hands on. A large man with a moustache was hogging the only copy of *The Times*.

Once seated, he read every word on the first three pages—from the date to the regional weather forecasts—but the words swam around his head in a mini-tornado. Not one sentence made sense. He flipped a few more pages, desperate for something to divert his thoughts.

Lord, he was seeing her in here too!

A picture of a model he'd just flicked past had made his stomach lurch. It was a bad idea to fuel his imagination when it was behaving like this, but he flipped the pages back anyway, and smoothed them down.

RISING FROM THE ASHES.

He didn't notice much of the other text apart from the headline. Something about a charity do. His eyes were fixed on the photo in the bottom right corner. *Rock star Damon Blade with Serendipity Dove,* the caption read.

Jake knew enough about the music scene to want to rip the head off the guy with his hand hooked around her waist. His gut clenched at the thought of it. Blade's mouth was only inches from her long, graceful neck as he whispered something in her ear. The tabloids called him a 'love rat', and by the look of him he was trying to take a nibble on Serena.

Look at him! He couldn't even take his eyes off her long enough to smile for the camera. But then, Jake could hardly blame him. She looked stunning, her eyes large and haunting, staring straight into the camera lens. Straight into his soul.

His heart stuttered.

It was as if she were looking right at him—which was ridiculous, of course. Blast that stupid brain of his! Always conjuring up things that weren't there. That was what had got him into this mess in the first place.

No matter. He still couldn't tear his eyes away from the picture. Even after almost two months he was hungry to see her. If a grainy print was all he could get hold of, it would have to do. He wondered if the waitress would shout at him if he tore it out and stuffed it in his pocket.

He looked back at the photo. She wasn't even smiling, really. Her eyes were sad, and her mouth and chin had a defiant set—issuing him a challenge, almost.

If you want me, come and get me—before it's too late.

He advised his clients to take risks, but he'd been guilty of ignoring his own good advice. He loved her, and hadn't she told him she loved him too? They were well suited—her warmth and impulsiveness a perfect complement to his over-analytical reserve. That sounded like a calculated risk, didn't it? Could it have worked?

No guarantees, he'd said. He'd been wrong. He was guaranteed one thing: he would regret it for the rest of his life if he didn't go and convince her to give him another chance.

The kitchen door crashed open and Serena looked up from her magazine. Cassie stood braced in the doorway. Body language like that normally meant trouble.

'We're on!' Cassie announced.

'I beg your pardon?'

'You heard. We're on—or at least you are. Saturday night at Lorenzo's, eight o'clock. You've got a date.'

Oh, flip!

She'd forgotten about her moment of insanity when she'd suggested Cassie start up the whole husband-hunt thing again. Trying to run before she could walk, she supposed.

Cassie sat opposite and leaned forward on her elbows. 'What's the matter? *You* asked me, remember?'

'I know. It's just—'

'Don't tell me you actually agreed to go out with Damon the Dastardly? I know he's phoned you three times a day since the party, but still!'

She shot Cass a *what-kind-of-idiot-do-you-think-I-am?* look. 'No, I'm not seeing Damon.' The very thought made her flesh crawl.

'So what's stopping you, then?'

Serena toyed with her mug of coffee.

'Exactly!' said Cassie, a triumphant gleam in her eye. 'Nothing.'

'I'm just not ready.'

'Nonsense. Time to get back on the horse, plenty more fish in the sea, every dog has its day—that sort of thing.'

Her cheeks creased into a smile. Cassie was priceless when she did her schoolmarm bit. 'Horses, fish, dogs? He's not a zookeeper, by any chance, is he?'

'No. Stop stalling.'

'So spill the beans. Who is candidate number four hundred and twenty-two?'

'Mr Right, of course.'

Sure.

She flapped her magazine closed. 'I really don't want to, Cass.'

'This was your idea, sweetie. You can't back out now! It's going to make me look stupid. Just go and have dinner with the man. If you don't like him, don't see him again. And I promise I won't set you up on any more dates for a few weeks.'

'Months.' Years.

'Okay, for a few months.' Cassie's smirk was the biggest one Serena had ever seen her wear, and that was saying something!

'So, who *is* Mr Right, then?'

'All you need to know is that he's tall, good-looking, and perfect for you.'

How many times had she heard that before?

'We'll see.'

The reflection in the glass of the restaurant door didn't look great. Her hair was wavy on one side and straight the other. Her fingers curled around the door handle. It seemed a lifetime away since she'd been standing here ready to meet a different stranger.

This meant nothing, really. She wouldn't even see the guy again. She was doing it to prove something to herself—a symbolic act to show that there was hope for the future. Far, far into the future.

'Are you gonna stand there all night, love?'

She jumped, and her fingers sprang away from the door handle as if it were red-hot. 'Sorry,' she mumbled, hardly looking at the man who barged past her into Lorenzo's.

Oh, get a grip!

She nipped inside before the door swung shut, and marched herself up to the bar.

'Hi, Gino.'

'Hey, *bambino*!' His eyes twinkled. 'Looking for love again?'

Serena snorted. 'How's Maria?'

'Good. She's in the back at the moment. I'd go and

get her for a chat, but we don't want to keep your fella waiting, do we?'

'He's not my *fella*.'

Gino just smiled.

The man who'd barged past her on his way in collected a couple of carrier bags from Marco, the chef—who winked at her—and swept back past her on his way out. At least he wasn't her date. A bucketload of fun that would have been!

Gino herded her towards the main part of the restaurant. She turned the corner and stopped.

'It's empty!'

Gino chuckled behind her. She spun round to look at him.

'It's Saturday night. You should be packed!'

He shrugged. 'Your fella wanted a little privacy.'

Oh, great! A date with a first-class bunny boiler. Her eyes darted around the room and she did a quick calculation of how many seconds it would take her to reach the exit if things went pear-shaped.

'Where is he, then?' When she'd said the room was empty, she hadn't been joking.

Gino led her to a table—her favourite table, the one she'd sat at waiting for Jake.

'Could I sit somewhere else, please?'

Gino shook his head.

'The place is deserted! Surely it wouldn't matter?'

'The gentleman was very specific.' He pulled out a chair and she dropped into it, scowling. She was still in the same pose when Gino returned with two glasses of champagne.

This was a bad sign. She hadn't even met the guy and he was already getting on her nerves. Far too smooth by half!

'Where's this Mr Wonderful, then?'

Gino just winked at her and turned to smile at Maria, who was now behind the bar, hands clasped, eyes shimmering.

She pushed the champagne glass away. 'Could you bring

me a mineral water, please, Gino?' She wasn't touching a drop of anything alcoholic until she knew it was safe to let her guard down. Gino disappeared, and she stared at the tablecloth. Her date was obviously building up to a grand entrance, and that did not bode well. It told her he thought he was the icing on the cake. The last thing she needed in her life at the moment was a man addicted to drama.

She traced the pattern in the tablecloth with her finger. Gino was a long time getting her water. She craned her neck to see what he was doing, but she only had a partial view of the bar, and he and Maria were nowhere to be seen.

She guessed he wasn't too far away, because the uncharacteristic silence had been broken by music, billowing chords that stroked the tension out of her shoulders. She smiled to herself as she imagined her date jumping out of a giant cake when the music reached its crescendo. There was something about this evening that was decidedly surreal.

Oh, well. She took a sip of champagne anyway—more for something to do than anything else. Mmm. Just another small sip.

She stilled and put down her glass. That vocal…it was so like…Max! That was Max's voice! What on earth…?

She tipped her head to one side and listened carefully. What was that he was singing? Something about being too scared to let a girl into his heart. It was beautiful. A sad tale of lost love and missed chances. She tried desperately not to mist over. Stupid, really, it just reminded her so much of what had gone wrong between her and Jake, as if he was singing their story.

When the instrumental break arrived she gave herself a stern talking-to. It would not be good if she was all red and puffy when Mr Right arrived. She swiped away some moisture with her finger and sniffed. Then, one by one, all the hairs on the back of her neck stood on end.

She didn't only recognise the voice; she recognised the tune. It was Jake's song! The one he'd played her in his flat the night he'd cooked her dinner. She just hadn't realised because with the other instruments and vocals it sounded fuller, more complete.

And now Max was singing about how he wanted to love her for ever, to have and to hold, to cherish her and never let her go.

Tears rolled down her cheeks, but she was too lost in the song to remember to wipe them away. Then the final chords wove themselves together and faded. She reached for her glass, but her fingers trembled too much to risk picking it up.

'I finished it.'

Her head jolted up and there he was—Jake. She grabbed onto the table, sure the world had just rolled on its axis.

'I discovered all I needed was a little inspiration.' He was walking towards her, trying to smile, but a little nerve twitched in his cheek. '*You* are my inspiration, Serendipity Dove. I needed *you* to make it complete.' He arrived at the table and sat opposite her, all the time keeping eye contact. She needed to remember to breathe every few seconds, she really did.

He took her hand. 'I need you to make *me* complete too.'

That was it. The tears fell like torrential rain. Those clear blue eyes were full of everything she had ever wanted to see in them. She tugged at the elaborately folded napkin in front of her, intending to bury her face in it.

Something flew out as she pulled it open, and tumbled onto her lap. Her fingers reached for it. She looked at him and he swallowed.

Her fingertips brushed against velvet. She grasped it and pulled a little jewellery box from under the table into the light. The air around them fizzed with static electricity. She was still staring at the box when she realised Jake had moved.

He was close beside her, but not touching. She met his gaze at eye level.

He was down on one knee.

A shiver ran right through her and the little box slid from her fingers. Jake was ready. He caught it in one deft swipe and held it out to face her. Her eyes grew wide as he eased the lid open.

Inside was a stunning antique ring. A square-cut emerald flanked by diamonds set in white gold. She couldn't have imagined anything more perfect.

His face went slightly grey. 'Serendipity Dove—I won't call you Serena; it's not your name, and it's the real you I love—will you marry me?'

He lifted the ring from its velvet cushion and held it near the tip of her finger, waiting.

Finally her tongue remembered what it was for! 'But you don't want me!'

'I want you more than anything in this world.'

She shook her head. 'You left.'

His eyes clouded over and a shadow passed over his face. 'I'm so sorry.' His thumb reached up and brushed the tears from her cheek. 'I thought I was being noble, but actually I was just being very, very stupid. I thought I was saving you from me. I knew you were desperate for the whole package, husband and babies, and I couldn't steal that dream from you, so I left.'

'But now you're back?'

'Yes. To stay, for ever—if you'll have me.'

If she'd thought her heart was beating fast before, now it doubled its efforts and sprinted off into the sunset.

'I thought you didn't *do* that kind of thing.'

'Only for you.'

She shook her head. This was all too much. She wanted to believe him, she really did, but he'd bolted on her twice before.

'Look at me.'

His deep blue eyes were earnest. She could see right inside, and there wasn't a shred of doubt or fear in them. 'I love you like I've never loved anyone else. I want to spend the next fifty years with you—or sixty, or seventy. I want to fight about who has the remote control and whose turn it is to change the next stinky nappy. I want you to remind me where I've left my false teeth when we're old and crusty. Please marry me. Say yes.'

She blinked, hardly daring to believe it was true. She'd better answer before this lovely dream evaporated.

'Yes. Yes, I'll marry you—*Charlie*.'

She half expected him to wince, understanding now why he hated his name, but he was the one who'd started being picky on the subject. He laughed, a deep guttural sound, and slipped the ring on. It sat comfortably there, as if her finger had always been waiting for it.

And then they were standing, and she was in his arms, his lips pressed against hers, and she thought she was going to pass out from sheer delight.

Slowly, she became aware of other noises in the room: whispers, shuffling, and then, growing in volume, a round of applause. She pulled away and stared at the dozen or so people gathered near the bar.

'Cass! Dad! Mel? All of you! What are you doing here?'

Jake whispered in her ear. 'I hired the restaurant for our engagement party.'

She punched him on the arm. 'You were a little sure of yourself, weren't you?'

'Actually, no. I knew I'd hurt you badly, and I had no idea what you'd say. I was prepared to look like a fool in front of all of them if you made a different decision. I was so fixated on the idea I was going to repeat my father's history I didn't give *us* a chance. I didn't try to prove myself wrong. I'm sorry.'

Champagne corks popped in the background, but she didn't move her eyes from his face. 'I was stubborn too! It wasn't all your fault. I had this picture-perfect idea of my future, and I wouldn't accept anything that didn't fit the template. It was stupid. At first all I saw was your suit and your job, but then I fell in love with you and it didn't matter what you wore or what you did. I just wanted you—any way I could have you.'

'And now you've got me. I hope you realise there's a no returns policy?'

'Oh, shut up and kiss me.'

She pulled him close by the lapels and savoured the taste and the feel of him. She was home.

Someone in the room let out a wolf whistle—probably Cass. They pulled apart, grinning.

'I suppose we'd better go and say hello to all our guests. After all, they made this possible.'

She looked at him, eyebrows raised.

'Cass was a mine of helpful information—and, of course, got you to turn up. Your dad and Max have worked round the clock for the last few days, helping me put down the song. I finished it on the plane journey back to London. It's amazing how much clarity you get when you're racing through the air, hoping to high heaven that you haven't messed up the best thing that ever happened to you.'

'The song is wonderful. You're wonderful. I love you so much.'

Then the crowd descended on them, and there was much hugging and kissing and slapping on backs. Mel was in tears, and Cass was grinning away as if she was responsible for the whole thing—which she was, of course, but it would never do to admit that. Her head was far too large already.

Finally, they found each other again. Their fingers laced together and he smiled down at her. She sighed. She wanted so much to be alone with him, away from all the chatter and clamour.

He read her look and his pupils grew.

'Later,' he whispered, and placed a kiss in the hollow beneath her ear. 'We've got the rest of our lives.'

nocturne™

WAS HE HER SAVIOR
OR HER NIGHTMARE?

HAUNTED
LISA CHILDS

Years ago, Ariel and her sisters were separated for
their own protection. Now the man who vowed
revenge on her family has resumed the hunt, and
Ariel must warn her sisters before it's too late.
The closer she comes to finding them, the more
secretive her fiancé becomes. Can she trust the man
she plans to spend eternity with? Or has he been
waiting for the perfect moment to destroy her?

On sale December 2006.

SNHDEC

SPECIAL EDITION™

Silhouette Special Edition brings you a heartwarming new story from the *New York Times* bestselling author of *McKettrick's Choice*

LINDA LAEL MILLER

Sierra's Homecoming

Sierra's Homecoming follows the parallel lives of two McKettrick women, living their lives in the same house but generations apart, each with a special son and an unlikely new romance.

December 2006

Visit Silhouette Books at www.eHarlequin.com   SSESHIBC

REQUEST YOUR FREE BOOKS!

2 FREE NOVELS PLUS 2
FREE GIFTS!

H A R L E Q U I N   R O M A N C E®

From the Heart, For the Heart

YES! Please send me 2 FREE Harlequin Romance® novels and my 2 FREE gifts. After receiving them, if I don't wish to receive any more books, I can return the shipping statement marked "cancel." If I don't cancel, I will receive 4 brand-new novels every month and be billed just $3.57 per book in the U.S., or $4.05 per book in Canada, plus 25¢ shipping and handling per book and applicable taxes, if any*. That's a savings of over 15% off the cover price! I understand that accepting the 2 free books and gifts places me under no obligation to buy anything. I can always return a shipment and cancel at any time. Even if I never buy another book from Harlequin, the two free books and gifts are mine to keep forever.

114 HDN EEV7   314 HDN EEWK

Name	(PLEASE PRINT)	
Address		Apt.
City	State/Prov.	Zip/Postal Code

Signature (if under 18, a parent or guardian must sign)

Mail to Harlequin Reader Service®:

IN U.S.A.	**IN CANADA**
P.O. Box 1867	P.O. Box 609
Buffalo, NY	Fort Erie, Ontario
14240-1867	L2A 5X3

Not valid to current Harlequin Romance subscribers.

Want to try two free books from another line?
Call 1-800-873-8635 or visit www.morefreebooks.com.

* Terms and prices subject to change without notice. NY residents add applicable sales tax. Canadian residents will be charged applicable provincial taxes and GST. This offer is limited to one order per household. All orders subject to approval. Credit or debit balances in a customer's account(s) may be offset by any other outstanding balance owed by or to the customer. Please allow 4 to 6 weeks for delivery.

HR06

COMING NEXT MONTH

#1846 IN HER BOSS'S ARMS—Elizabeth Harbison
Laurel Midland is excited about her new job as nanny to a motherless girl with a wealthy but distant father. On her first day, Charles Gray tells her to leave—he wants an older nanny. But Laurel stays, and it isn't long before Charles begins to fall under her spell….

#1847 FALLING FOR THE FRENCHMAN—Claire Baxter
Beth has struggled to get over old love Pierre Laroche, but now he's back, and this time it's to take over her beloved Barossa Valley winery. Beth knows she should hate Pierre, but glimpses of the man she loved ten years ago can still be seen under the cynical businessman….

#1848 HER READY-MADE FAMILY—Jessica Hart
Successful city hotshot Morgan Steele has decided her life is empty—so she gives up her career to move to the country! Handsome neighbor Alistair Brown believes she is a spoiled city girl, but as the attraction between them grows, Morgan realizes he might be everything she's looking for….

#1849 RESCUE AT CRADLE LAKE—Marion Lennox
Top surgeon Fergus Reynard left the city for a GP's life at Cradle Lake, hoping to soothe his broken heart. Ginny Viental is just what he is looking for and Fergus would do anything to make a life with her, even if it means taking on a role he thought he would never face again—that of a father.